FURY

THE CHAOS DEMONS MC
NICOLA JANE

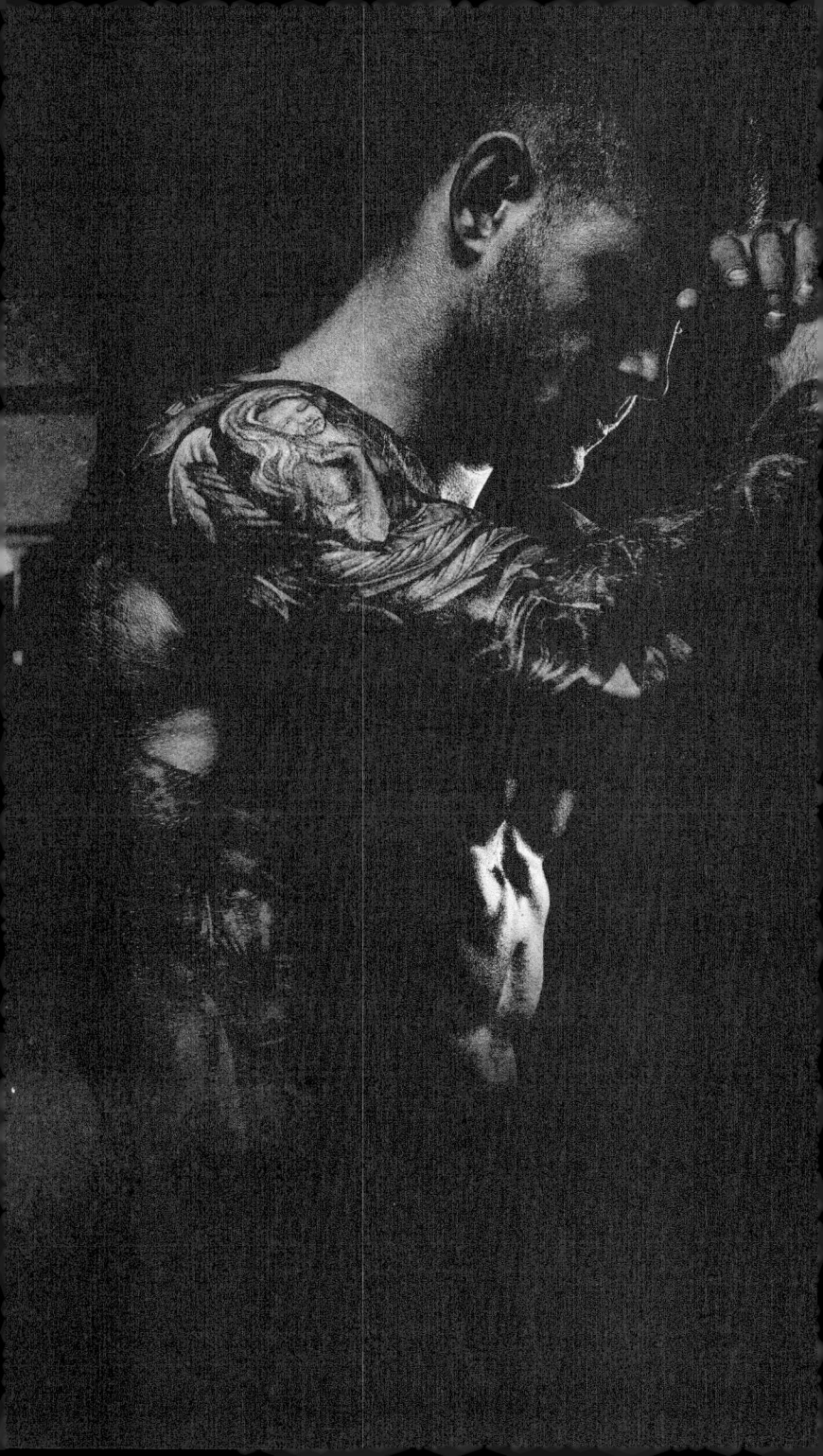

Copyright © 2025
Fury
The Chaos Demons MC
By Nicola Jane

All rights are reserved.
No part of this
book may be used or reproduced in any manner without written permission from the author,
except in the case of brief quotations used in articles or reviews. For information, contact Nicola Jane.

No AI has been used in creating the cover or contents of this book.

This book is a work of fiction. The names, characters, places, and incidents are all products of the author's imagination and are not to be construed as real. Any similarities are entirely coincidental.

Cover Designer: Wingfield Designs
Editor: Rebecca Vazquez, Dark Syde Books
Proofreader: Jackie Ziegler, Dark Syde Books
Formatting: V.R. Formatting

SPELLING NOTE

Please note, this author resides in the United Kingdom and is using British English. Therefore, some words may be viewed as incorrect or spelled incorrectly, however, they are not.

TRIGGER WARNING

This book contains triggers for violence, explicit scenes, and some dirty talking bikers. If any of this offends you, put your concerns in writing to Axel, he'll get back to you . . . maybe.

ACKNOWLEDGMENTS

Thank you to all my wonderful readers—you rock!

PLAYLIST:

Million Years Ago - Adele
When We Were Young – Adele
Hello – Adele
Until I Found You – Stephen Sanchez
Iris – Goo Goo Dolls
Someone You Loved – Lewis Capaldi
Birds Of a Feather – Billie Eilish
Nonsense – Sabrina Carpenter
Single Ladies (Put a Ring on It) – Beyoncé
Unchained Melody – Norah Jones
Lover – Taylor Swift
'03 Bonnie & Clyde – Jay-Z ft. Beyoncé
Stand by You – Rachel Platten
Love Me For The Both Of Us – CJ Fam
we can't be friends (wait for your love) – Ariana Grande
The Way – Ariana Grande ft. Mac Miller

CHAPTER 1

Fury

I try to prise my swollen eyes open, catching a glimpse of Chevy as his fist slams into my stomach. I wince, but not enough for him to notice. *Pussy*. "Untie me and try that," I spit.

He laughs, stepping back and making way for his boss, Donnie Nelson, to stand before me. "You lost me a lot of money tonight," he drawls.

"I fucked up," I snap, tugging hard on my restraints. "Arrange another fight and I'll stick to the rules."

He's already rolling up his shirt sleeves, and I brace myself for his onslaught, but right as he raises his arm, the door swings open, grabbing everyone's attention. I can just about make out the Chaos Demons kutte, but my relief is short-lived when Pit steps closer. He loves to drag shit out, and I'm out of time. "Don't stop on my account," he says, grinning.

"Did you see what he fucking did out there?" rages Donnie. "Where the hell is your President?"

"I saw," says Pit, casually leaning against the wall. "And if you want to speak with my President, Donnie, you gotta put in for a meet." Donnie scoffs and turns back to me. "Before you continue," Pit cuts in, "I should remind you that if you hurt one brother, you hurt us all."

"He fucked the night up," Donnie yells.

"And you're pissed, I get that, but we all know Fury didn't get his name for being a pushover. If your man couldn't withstand the hits, you should've backed the right horse."

I hear the click of a gun and groan. This is going from bad to worse. Pit smirks like he doesn't have a care in the world. "My President would like to propose a deal," he drawls. *A deal? A fucking deal?* "Fury will work the debt off, but from now on, there will be no more throwing fights where Fury is concerned."

"You think your President holds any weight down here in my fucking ring?" Donnie bellows. "He can't even come here and make the deal face to face!"

"Because Fury will fight for you. He'll make you more money than you've ever made."

I glare at Pit, but through the swelling, he doesn't notice and continues to stare at Donnie, waiting for his next move. "And what if he doesn't win?" he barks.

"That's not an option," says Pit. "Besides, aren't we down here because he refused to lose? Do we have a deal or not?"

Donnie hits me in the ribs, and I cry out. It's the exact same spot I was hit in the fight, and I've definitely broken a couple. I see Pit's fist curl. It's not in his nature to stand back and watch a brother get beat on, but right now, with a gun pointing at him, he's got no choice. "Deal," Donnie snaps, turning for the door.

Once he's gone, Pit turns to Chevy. "You're lucky your

bitch ass has a gun," he hisses. "Now, untie him and get the fuck outta my sight."

I feel the rope on my wrists fall away, and I force myself to my feet, despite my ribs protesting, and square up to Chevy, who smirks. "One day," I warn.

Pit grabs me by the shirt and shoves me towards the door. "Don't you think you're in enough shit right now?" he hisses.

We battle through the crowd gathering to watch the next fight and break out into the cool evening air, where Pit spins on me. "What the fuck were you thinking?"

I grin. "I wasn't."

"Axel is losing his head. You better get back there and face the music."

AXEL DOESN'T LET ME SPEAK UNTIL HE'S HIT ME SQUARE IN THE face. "Fuck," I hiss, cupping my jaw.

"You went behind my back," he roars, pushing me onto the desk and pinning me there. "You crossed into Donnie's territory, where you know we can't fucking go, and then you fight in his club!"

"It was a lapse in judgement," I admit.

Grizz pulls Axel from me, and I stand fully, straightening my shirt. "A lapse in judgment is shooting too much whiskey," Grizz mutters, slapping Axel on the back as he goes to sit behind his desk.

"What were you thinking?" Axel asks.

"You got a death wish?" asks Grizz.

I stare down at the ground, cos if he looks me in the eye, he'll see that's exactly what I went in that ring with tonight. I was looking for an easy way out.

"Look," says Axel, sighing heavily, "you transferred here from Nottingham to get a fresh start. You've been here a month and you're already causing me shit."

"Don't send me back," I mutter, cos the last thing I need is to face the music there.

"Then sort your shit out," says Grizz firmly. "We don't need a war with Donnie right now."

"You owe him thirty grand," says Axel, and my head whips up in surprise.

"He bet thirty grand on that streaky piece of piss?"

"Well, that streaky piece of piss happened to be his nephew," says Axel. "You were told you'd get ten grand to throw that fight, and you didn't, so now, you owe him."

"I don't have that kind of money," I admit. "Not right now."

"Lucky for you, he doesn't want your money. He wants your time."

"What's that mean?" I ask.

"It means until further notice, you're his new bitch. Be at this address at seven a.m. tomorrow." Axel slides me a piece of paper with an address scribbled down. "And you'll feature in his fights, which you'll win. He'll take a sixty-forty split, and if you don't win, that'll add on to the debt."

"Are you fucking joking me?" I snap. "It'll never end."

"That's the price you've gotta pay," says Grizz.

"Or we could just end the stupid fucker," I suggest.

"I'm not going to war with an organised crime gang because you couldn't follow my orders," says Axel. "So, you'll keep your head down and get on with it until further notice."

Grizz heads for the door. "Come on, I'll drop you at the hospital to get checked."

I groan. "Can't I just see the club doc?"

"Nope, you can sit in accident and emergency for a few hours and think about the shit you've caused," snaps Axel.

It's two hours before I'm called through to be assessed by the nurse. Two hours of people staring at me and whispering because of the kutte, always assuming the worst.

The receptionist points to a room, and I step inside. The nurse behind the curtain is just putting on new gloves, and when she looks up at me, my whole world slows. I stare open-mouthed as she smiles wide. "Oh my god, Reese Northman?"

It's been so long since anyone used my real name, it takes me a second to respond. "Xanthe May Hart," I murmur, ignoring the way my heart beats wildly in my chest.

Xanthe

It's been a long time, but I'd know that face anywhere, even with the bruising. The last time I saw it, my heart was breaking—not because of anything he did, but because he was moving away, and it was out of our control.

I break out of the trance-like stare we're currently locked in and throw my arms around him. He hisses, and I immediately pull back. "Oh shit, sorry. Of course, you're hurt, why else would you be here?" I ask, adding a laugh and running my eyes over his bruised face. "What the hell happened?"

"A long story."

I frown. "And I have time, so lie on the bed and lift your shirt."

He eases himself onto the bed and slowly lies back. "How have you been?" he asks.

I push his shirt up and arch a brow. "Broken ribs," I confirm, "but you'll need an X-ray."

"How come you're in London?" he asks.

"Stare at my face," I tell him, leaning closer and shining a torch in each eye. His pupils dilate. "What happened?"

"I fight," he says casually. "No big deal."

"You lost this one, I take it."

He smirks. "I never lose."

"You're telling me the other guy came off worse than this?" I ask, laughing.

"How have you been, Xanth?" he asks again, this time with that little lost boy look in his eye.

I gently run my hand over his cheek. "Good. How about you?"

"Good."

"You're in The Chaos Demons," I note, staring at the club patch on his jacket. They're well known around here, especially to us emergency workers.

"They keep me in line," he says, a smile playing on his lips.

"And they keep us busy. It's mainly just cuts and bruises," I tell him, "but I'd like to have your ribs X-rayed."

He's already pushing to sit up. "I'm all good. Save the NHS some money." I gently push him back down, and he smirks. "Still trying to be dominant, I see," he says, and I feel myself blushing.

"Let me at least clean up your face." I pull the bed light down over him and drag my tray of implements closer. I'm not ready for him to walk out of here without having properly spoken. I begin to wash out a cut above his eyebrow, and he winces. "So, are you married?" I ask.

He laughs. "No. You?"

I'm surprised at his answer. He's good looking and has the personality to match. Even as a naughty teenager, he was funny and made anything seem possible. He always had girls swooning over him. "No, not married."

He looks just as surprised. "You remember we made a pact, right?" he reminds me, and I laugh as I use gauze to pat the eyebrow dry.

"You were always making pacts and promises. How many

girls did you promise to marry if they were still single by thirty-five?"

His smile fades. "Just the one, Xanth." The look in his eye is so serious, I have to turn away to compose myself.

"Glue should hold this cut, but if it continues to bleed, come back for stitches." I carefully glue his cut and hold it together for a few seconds.

"What time do you get off work?" he asks.

My heart slams harder in my chest as I glance at my watch. "In half an hour."

"I'll wait."

"What for?"

"You," he says simply.

"THIS IS CRAZY, RIGHT?" I whisper to my friend and colleague, Julianna.

"Yes, but all the best things are. He's just an old friend."

I stare back at the cubicle where Reese is waiting for me. "But I've met someone."

"You're freaking out, Xanth, and getting way ahead of yourself as usual. This is just a catch-up. He might turn out to be a right knob, and you'll be texting, asking me to get you out of there."

I give a stiff nod even though I already know she's wrong. I've thought about Reese Northman every day since the day he left me behind. "I've spent all this time looking for a man, and now, two come along at once."

Julianna rolls her eyes. "I could think of worse problems to have."

I slip my coat on and grab my bag. "I'll text you later," I tell her, air-kissing her cheek.

Reese is sitting on the bed staring at his mobile phone. He glances up when I tug the curtain back. "Ready?" I ask.

He nods, shoving his mobile away and following me out.

We find a late-night café just two streets away and take a seat. "The good thing about London is places like this," I say. "You can never feel lonely when there are late-night cafés around."

He smiles. "I guess not."

"So, tell me where you've been."

His hood is up, hiding part of his face, and I wish he'd take it down so I can see his expression properly. I used to know when he was lying or hiding something, and right now, I long to see whether his eyes are filled with pain when he recalls his movements or if he's found happiness.

"From Manchester, I went to Liverpool, but the family there was too much, so I ran away to Nottingham. I got into some shit, ended up inside, and found the club. I came to London a month ago."

My heart aches knowing he didn't find the family he so deserved. "My mum always wondered where you ended up," I say.

"Yeah?" he asks, smiling. "How is she?"

I nod. "Good. Really good. She doesn't foster anymore. I had to convince her to take some time for herself after my dad died."

"Shit, Xanth, I'm so sorry."

"Don't be, it was sudden, so he didn't suffer." I take a breath. "Heart attack," I add, "five years ago."

"That's shit," he mutters.

"For what it's worth, he regretted what happened," I offer, not quite meeting his eyes, "just letting them take you away so suddenly."

He shifts uncomfortably in his seat. "It was a long time ago."

"What do you do now?" I ask, changing the subject.

"This and that," he says, smirking, and my heart sinks a little. My parents fostered hundreds of kids, wanting them to have a good start in life. Reese didn't work out, like lots of others, but knowing he's following the same pattern of behaviour his own parents did is sad. "And you're a nurse," he states. "I always knew you'd be helping people."

"You were good at that too," I remind him.

He looks away, grabbing a paper menu and scanning it. "I've changed a lot since then, Xanth."

"Maybe one day I can watch you fight," I suggest, even though I hate all that violence.

"Maybe."

A waitress bounces over, smiling wide at Reese. "Hey, Fury," she gushes. "What can I get you?"

"Usual," he replies. "And the same for my friend," he adds, nodding in my direction. She scans her eyes over me dismissively and saunters off.

"You've been here a month and you're already befriending the locals," I point out, amused.

"She's friends with someone in the club," he replies.

"Fury?" I repeat the name she used for him.

"Road name," he mutters.

"You never did like Reese."

"It was my dad's name," he reminds me.

The waitress returns with two coffees and places them on the table. "I get off in ten minutes," she says pointedly.

He gives a stiff nod, and she smiles wide and goes off to clear another table. The silence stretches between us, and I pull out my mobile to check for messages. There's just one, and when I open it, I smile.

CHAPTER 2

Fury

I stare at Xanthe from under my hood. She's just as beautiful as I remember. She never wore a lot of makeup because it just wasn't needed. Her blue eyes always shone bright, especially when she was happy, and I see that happiness now as she stares down at her mobile phone.

"Who's the lucky guy?" I ask casually.

She glances up, her cheeks reddening slightly before she tucks her mobile away. "Are you sticking around London?"

She was always good at changing the subject when she didn't want to answer a question. "As long as he's treating you good," I say, offering a small smile to let her know I see what she just did. "I'll be here for a few months at least," I reply, knowing it'll take me a lot longer to clear my debt to Donnie.

"We should spend some time together. You could come and see Mum."

The thought of seeing Dianna fills me with dread. We

parted on bad terms, not that Xanthe is aware of that. "Maybe," I say with a shrug. "Is she living in London?"

Xanthe nods enthusiastically. "We all moved to London years back. The need for foster carers is huge here, and you know what my parents were like. Plus, they wanted us to have better opportunities." She leans forward slightly, propping her elbows on the table and resting her chin on her hand. "I can't believe you're single, Reese Northman."

"Fury," I correct. "I sort of had someone," I admit, wincing at the ache in my heart. "Back in Nottingham. It didn't work out."

She offers a sympathetic smile. "Well, looks like your new . . . friend is waiting for you," she comments, looking past me to where Jennie is putting her jacket on. I don't bother to correct her. Jennie is a new club girl at the MC, and we just happened to gravitate toward each other with us both being newbies. She's good friends with London, and I often give her a ride home when she's on the late shifts.

"I could get her to wait here while I take you home first," I offer, suddenly regretting coming to this café.

Xanthe smiles as she stands. "It's fine. I don't live too far. Besides, I have a lift." She glances out the window as a car glides to a stop outside. She pulls out her mobile and hands it to me. "Put your number in, and I'll call you."

"Will you, though?" I ask, smirking as I input the information.

"Of course. We'll have dinner."

I nod, watching as she grabs her coat and bag and heads out to the waiting car. "Are you ready?" asks Jennie, hooking her arm through mine. "My feet are killing."

My alarm sounds, and I groan. My entire body aches, so

when Jennie rolls over and throws her leg over me, I push it off and sit up. "What time is it?" she groans.

"Early."

"Come back to bed," she murmurs, running her nails gently down my back.

I roll my eyes. I don't know how we've come to spending the nights together. It's something I keep vowing to stop, yet when it comes down to it, I can't quite kick her out.

I head for the shower, hoping she'll leave, but when I go back into the room, she's fast asleep. I sigh heavily. It's another thing in my life I need to get on top of.

BY THE TIME I GET TO THE ADDRESS AXEL GAVE ME, I'M irritated. What the fuck could Donnie possibly want me to do for him other than fight? I press the buzzer on the gates, and they slowly open. I drive up the gravel driveway and stop outside the show home, where Chevy is waiting for me with a grin on his face.

I pull off my helmet and dismount the bike, staring past him at the house. "He complained about thirty-grand, yet he lives here," I state.

Chevy laughs. "He's waiting for you inside."

I follow him in and through the house, down into the basement gym, where Donnie is pounding away on the running machine. He glances my way. "You came."

"Didn't really have a choice," I mutter.

"Your President was surprisingly keen to agree to my terms."

I roll my eyes. "It's temporary."

He laughs. "We'll see. Chevy will show you the ropes."

"What exactly will I be doing?"

He slows the machine down to a walk. "Whatever you're told."

I follow Chevy back upstairs, watching as he grabs a set of car keys. "We have a job at the fight club," he tells me.

"I can follow on my bike," I say as we head out to a sleek black SUV.

He shakes his head. "Not an option. Whilst you're here, you'll drive one of these cars out front." He gets into the driver's side, and I climb into the passenger side. "If I were you, I'd keep my head down and do as I'm told. The more you protest, the longer he'll have you cleaning up shit."

We arrive at the club and go through the back doors. The place is empty, and the smell of stale sweat is heavy. He unlocks a door at the back of the room, and we head down a set of stone steps. He turns on a light, and I wince at the sight of a bloodied male lying on a plastic sheet on the floor.

"The tools you need are there," says Chevy, pointing to a table of various saws and knives.

I frown. "What am I meant to do with that lot?"

He grins. "Cut him up," he says simply.

My eyes widen as I stare at the lifeless body. "Are you shitting me?"

He shakes his head and points to a barrel. "Put him in the acid. Gloves for that are on the table too." And then he turns around and goes back up the stairs. "I'll come back for you in an hour."

I stare down at the body in disbelief. It's not like I've not done my fair share of disposals, but we have a clean-up team in the MC, so it's been a while since I had to get my hands dirty. I groan, grabbing a saw from the table and dropping to my knees.

EACH SLICE PISSES ME OFF FURTHER. I DROP EACH BODY PART INTO the drum of acid, one by one until there's nothing left but the bloodied sheet. I add that into the drum and pull off my gloves, wiping my sweaty brow on the back of my hand. My mobile rings, and I see Axel's name. I accept and hold it to my ear.

"Pres," I greet.

"Just checking in."

"You wouldn't believe what I'm fucking doing," I spit, staring at the bloodied saw on the table. "Clean-up."

"Shit, he's really gonna make you pay. Who's he getting rid of?"

"Looks like it was a fight to the death," I mutter. It's not unheard of, but it's rare these days.

"Yeah, I heard rumours that he runs that kind of shit. He's a sick fucker, which is why I told you to avoid fighting in his club. Come and see me when you get back."

"Sure," I say on a sigh, disconnecting.

Xanthe

JORJA TUCKS INTO HER SALAD, WAITING FOR ME TO FILL HER IN. It's been over a week since we last met up, which is a long time for us, but I've been working extra shifts all week.

"He was sweet," I tell her.

She arches a brow. "The guy was loaded. He was in the VIP area. Did he at least kiss you?"

I laugh. "No."

"Ugh," she says, rolling her eyes.

"I didn't want him to kiss me," I say, shrugging. "I mean, not because I didn't fancy him, because I really did." We both laugh. "But I want him to be different, yah know?"

"A gentleman?" she asks.

"Yes," I say, relieved she gets me. "I'm so tired of men just after one thing. I'm ready now. I want the happily ever after."

"And you think rich guy could be it?"

I shrug, smiling when I think of the guy we met last week

on a night out. He was smooth yet sweet. "He's been texting me all week, and even made sure he got me a lift home on my late shift."

"Got you a lift?" she questions.

"He was working, so he sent one of his guys."

She smirks. "Wow. He has guys."

"Speaking of my late shift, I saw a really old friend. He came into the hospital all beat-up."

"Do I know him?" she asks.

I shake my head. "Reese Northman. He was from my teen years."

"Oh yeah?" she asks, wiggling her brows. "Didn't you say you were off the rails as a teen?"

"Wasn't everyone?" I tease. My smile fades as I think about Reese, or Fury, as he prefers now. "He was off the rails too. We were kind of off together."

"Friends or more?"

I grin. "More. But then he moved away, and I didn't hear from him again."

"Harsh. Did he break your heart?"

I think over her words, feeling that familiar twinge in my chest. "I think we broke each other's without meaning to."

"That's sad," she says, taking another mouthful of food. "What's he like now?"

I smile wider. "Fit."

She laughs out loud. "Are you seeing him again?"

"I took his number so we could catch up."

"Did you have sex with him?"

My mouth opens in mock horror. "I don't even know him anymore."

"I mean when you were teens," she says, rolling her eyes.

I nod. "Yeah."

"So, catching up might lead somewhere?"

I shake my head. "Nah, I doubt it. He's part of The Chaos Demons MC, for a start. He hasn't changed his ways."

"Hey," she defends, "that club ain't all bad. They do a lot of nice shit in the community."

"To cover up all the bad they do," I point out.

"Rumours," she says, shrugging. "People fear what they don't understand."

"And you understand?"

She laughs. "No, but they helped my mum once when she struggled to feed us. It wasn't the same guy in charge back then, but I think they live by the same morals." Jorja has lived in this area since she was born, so I'd expect her to defend the stories about the club and believe they're doing good in the local community.

"Either way, I don't know him anymore. I might call and ask him to dinner so we can catch up properly, but beyond that, he's just a kid I used to know."

When I get home, I shower and then decide to text Fury. It can't hurt to catch up and see what his life is like now. At the very least, I can fill Mum in.

> Me: Hi, it's Xanthe. Just wondering if you'd like to catch up sometime.

I hit send then groan. Why does it sound so *bothered/not bothered*? I shudder, but before I can analyse it further, his reply comes.

> Fury: Tonight. 8 p.m.

I frown. He's always been blunt and bossy.

> Me: Okay. Where?

> Fury: Your place.

> Me: Actually, I was thinking dinner might be nice.

> Fury: I'll bring food.

I sigh heavily, unsure how I feel about having a biker in my home. I laugh to myself. This is Reese. He'd never hurt me. But I don't reply with my address and instead decide that when he texts back to ask for it, I'll arrange to meet him at a bar.

I MUST HAVE DRIFTED OFF BECAUSE I WAKE WITH A START AND SIT up, looking around. I'm still wrapped in my towel from the shower, and my hair is damp. A loud bang makes me jump, and I get up off the bed and pull the blinds back from the bedroom window to see Fury at the front door. He looks up before I can step back, and I groan out loud. I can't exactly ignore him now, but how the fuck did he find my address?

I grab my dressing gown and swap it from the towel, then I head down to open up. He grins. "Thought you were hiding from me. I've been knocking for ages." He holds up a bag of what I assume is food. "I got Chinese."

"How did you get my address?" I ask as he steps past me and goes straight for the kitchen with me rushing after him.

"Plates?" he asks, and I point to the cupboard. "You just woke up?" he adds, looking me up and down.

I tug the robe tighter. "Erm, I must've fell asleep after my shower. I've been working a lot lately. I'll just go and get dressed." He nods, and I go upstairs, reeling with confusion.

I tug open my drawers and rummage through, trying to find something that's casual but not ugly. I settle on leggings and a short vest.

When I get back downstairs, Fury is sitting at the table,

tucking into a mix of Chinese on his plate. The containers are laying open on the table, and he points to my plate. "I wasn't sure what you wanted, but I remembered you like variety, so I grabbed plenty."

I smile as I take a seat and begin to spoon different things onto my plate. "It's weird," I state, and he pauses eating to look at me. "You haven't really changed, but at the same time, you have."

"That makes no sense," he replies, continuing to eat.

"You're acting like we were never apart," I state. And the words hit me hard as my mind conjures up a slideshow of the times I watched Reese shovel food into his mouth like he was starved. When he came to us, he would grab it up in his hands like someone was about to snatch it from him. It used to break my heart.

He stares at me for a few silent minutes. "It doesn't feel like we were."

I stare down at my food. "You never came to say goodbye."

"Drink?" he asks, pushing to his feet and heading for the fridge. He retrieves two bottles of beer that I assume he brought with him.

"You still hate to talk," I point out.

He places a bottle in front of me and unscrews the cap. "What's there to say? It was a long time ago, and I can't remember it."

"Really?" I push. "None of it?"

He shrugs as he lowers back into his seat. "Tell me about your life now, Xanth."

I sigh, hating that I've let myself cloud this reunion with bad memories, memories that until now, I'd managed to squash. "I've been nursing for ten years," I say. "I love it."

"Boyfriend?"

"Can you stop doing that?" I ask briskly, and he glances

up again, this time placing his fork down. "You just keep firing words at me like you're interrogating me."

He swallows the food in his mouth. "Sorry." And I see a glimpse of the vulnerable kid I once knew. "Habit."

"I met someone, but it's very early days," I admit. "What about you and the waitress?"

He shakes his head. "We're not a thing. She's a . . . a club girl."

"What does that mean?"

"She hangs around the club and spends time with the guys . . . any of them. She doesn't belong to one particular biker."

I wince in disgust. "Nice," I say sarcastically.

"I don't expect someone like you to understand," he mutters.

I frown. "Someone like me?"

He shrugs. "Maybe this was a bad idea." He stands, and I follow him with my eyes. "And for what it's worth, I never wanted to leave you the way I did."

CHAPTER 3

Fury

"We need to go to the hospital and pick someone up," says Chevy the following day.

I check my watch. It's almost nine in the evening, and I've spent the entire day cleaning up the shit caused by him and Donnie. I've still got to get to the gym and do my two-hour workout. Chevy notices and grins. "Don't stress, I'll drop you back to the club after."

He pulls out into traffic. "Maybe I should've set an hourly rate," I tell him. "I have a feeling the debt would be paid much sooner."

He laughs. "That's what you think. Donnie will keep you working until he decides otherwise."

Ten minutes later, we pull to a stop around the back of the hospital. "Open the back door for her," says Chevy. I glance at my blood-soaked jeans. "She won't even notice," he mutters.

"Who are we picking up, anyway?" I hiss, climbing out the car.

"Some bitch Donnie is trying to impress," he replies.

I round the car and pull open the back door right as the hospital's fire exit doors open and Xanthe walks out. She doesn't look up from rummaging in her bag as she slides into the car, and I slam the door with my heart racing in my chest. *What the fuck is she involved in?*

I get back into the passenger front seat and stare straight ahead. "Good shift?" asks Chevy politely.

"Yeah. Long but busy. You really don't need to keep picking me up. I keep telling Donnie it's not necessary."

Chevy gives a light chuckle, and it's so far from the guy I know, I almost break my cover to call him out on it. "He doesn't like to think of you walking in the dark."

She laughs. "I've been doing it a long time."

Chevy's phone lights up, and he hands it to me. "It's the boss," he mutters.

I have no choice but to answer, and the second I say, "Hello," I feel her eyes burn into mine through the rearview mirror.

"Bring Xanthe to the club," snaps Donnie. "It's urgent." He disconnects, and I place the mobile back in the holder.

"He wants you to take her straight to the club."

"Reese?" she murmurs, and I glare at her in the mirror, giving my head a slight shake. If they know we know one another, Donnie might try and use that. And when I get her the hell away from him, which I plan to do as soon as possible, he'll definitely put a bullet in me.

"Who's Reese?" asks Chevy.

I glance back at Xanthe and grin. "Oh shit, sorry, I didn't recognise you." Then I turn to Chevy, who looks confused. "She was the nurse who dealt with me the other night after my fight."

Xanthe gathers herself and forces a smile. "I'm glad to see the glue held that cut."

"Yep. All good now, thanks."

"Why does Donnie want me to go to him?" she asks. "He doesn't usually."

"No idea," I say casually. "He just said it was urgent."

We arrive at the boxing club, and I round the car to open her door. Chevy joins us, and we walk in together, pushing people out the way to make room for her. We see Lester waving from the office doorway, so I guide Xanthe that way. My heart is slamming so hard in my chest, I can hardly hear the crowd as they cheer on the current fighters. Xanthe looks around frantically, and I gently slip my hand into hers and give it a reassuring squeeze before releasing it again.

Lester opens the office door, and Donnie is pacing back and forth. He stops as we step into the office, rushing to Xanthe and pulling her into his arms. "I'm so sorry to bring you here like this."

"What's going on?" she asks, and I notice a slight waver in her voice.

"You know I wouldn't normally involve you, but this kid, he's . . . important to me." He steps back, keeping his arm around Xanthe. There's a beat-up teenager slouched in the corner, and Xanthe inhales sharply. "He got involved in something, and I can't send him home like that." He leads her closer, and the teen stirs. "Can you patch him up?"

"He should really go to the hospital, Donnie," she says, shaking her head.

"And I promise I'll have his mum take him, but before that, can you check him over so I can tell her he's okay?"

I see the internal battle she's having with herself before eventually nodding. "Okay."

I inwardly groan as Donnie pulls out a bag of first aid stuff. "Thanks, I appreciate it." Donnie pats Chevy on the shoulder. "Can we go for a chat?" Then, he turns to me. "Wait with her and come find me when she's done." I give a slight nod, opening the door for them to leave.

I stay by the door as she tends to the kid. After a few

minutes, she turns back to look at me. "What's going on?" she hisses.

"I have no idea," I say blankly, staring at the wall opposite me.

"Reese," she snaps.

"Fury," I correct her.

She marches over until I have no choice but to look at her. "Do you work for Donnie?"

"Are you fucking him?" I growl, surprised how bitter the words sound out loud.

"Stop answering my questions with a question," she demands.

"Do what he's asked you to do," I mutter, looking back to the opposite wall. "He can't know we know each other."

"Why?"

"He just can't," I snap, and she jumps at my words before slowly backing up and tending to the kid.

Once she's done, she stands fully. "He's got concussion," she tells me.

"I'll get Donnie," I mutter, opening the office door to find him just a few feet away. He looks my way, and I wave for him to come over. "She's all done," I tell him.

He comes into the office and runs his eyes over the kid. "Is he okay?"

"Concussed," Xanthe replies. "He needs rest and regular painkillers."

"Perfect. No lasting damage then?"

"I don't know about that. He needs to see a doctor ASAP."

"Yeah, yeah, I'll arrange that." He slides his hand over Xanthe's cheek, and I drop my eyes to the ground as he places a gentle kiss on her lips. "Thank you for sorting this, babe. I'll make it up to you. Fury will take you home." He throws me the car keys.

"I can walk," she mutters.

"Xanthe," he says firmly until she meets his eye, "go with Fury. He's a pussy cat."

She gives a stiff nod and follows me from the room. Outside, I open the car door, and she slides into the back seat. I get into the driver's seat and start the engine. It's only as I pull into traffic that I hear her softly crying to herself. My heart twists painfully, just like it used to whenever she was upset. *Fuck*. It's like we've never been apart.

I slow outside her house, and before I can open her door, she jumps out and rushes up the path. I groan, getting out and following her. She slams the door in my face, and I rest my forehead against it. "Xanth, come on," I plead.

"Go away."

"Please."

The door swings open, and I stare at her red, puffy eyes. "Why are you covered in blood?"

I glance down at my clothes. "Long story."

She growls in frustration and tries to slam the door again, only this time, I wedge my foot there and it bounces back. "We should talk inside," I insist, stepping in and forcing her back a few steps. I slam the door. "How the fuck did you get involved with Donnie?" I demand.

"No," she yells, stomping into the kitchen with me hot on her heels. "I'm not answering any more of your questions until you start talking."

"He's bad news," I snap.

"As are you?" She says it more like a question.

"I'm serious, Xanth."

"So am I. Do you work for him?"

I briefly close my eyes and release a sigh. "No. I owe him money, and I'm paying off my debt."

"How?"

"By doing whatever he wants."

"Like?"

"Like picking his piece of ass up from work," I yell.

She looks offended. "I hardly know him," she shouts angrily. "And I am no one's piece of ass."

I give a nod, relief flooding me. "Great, so you can walk away?"

She narrows her eyes. "Hold on a minute, who said anything about walking away?"

"Me," I snap. "I'm telling you to walk away before you get too involved. That show tonight, that'll happen again and again. Now he knows you'll do it, he'll call on you."

"I'll make it clear I'm not doing it again."

I scoff. "And you think he'll take any notice?"

"He can't force me," she shouts.

I grab her upper arms and shake her. "He's a fucking psycho. You need to listen to me."

"You're the only one acting crazy," she snaps, pulling her arms free. "Why are you covered in blood?" she asks again.

"Walk away from him, Xanth, or one day, it might be your blood I'm covered in."

She stares at me for a long, silent minute before giving a stiff nod. I exhale, relief flooding me.

"I'll send him a text." She pulls out her mobile. "What should I say?"

"Just be honest," I tell her.

She types something out then turns the phone for me to see.

> I'm really sorry, but I think we should call it a day. This isn't going to work for me.

I nod, and she presses send. Seconds later, his reply comes, and she groans, showing me the phone again.

> Donnie: I'm coming over now to talk.

"Fuck," I mutter. "Text him back quickly and tell him you're going to bed or something."

"I'll talk to him," she says with a shrug, "make him see it won't work. You should go."

"I don't think that's a good idea," I begin, but she's already shaking her head.

"I'll be fine. Honestly, he's been so sweet to me."

"Be careful," I mutter, rubbing my thumb over her cheek. I lean closer, placing a gentle kiss on her forehead. She closes her eyes, inhaling sharply. "Text me when he's gone so I know you're okay."

It takes everything I have to leave her there. Donnie is a slimy fucker, and I have no doubt he'll convince her to give them a try.

Xanthe

Donnie has never been to my place, so when I open the door and he steps inside, it feels foreign. We always meet at a restaurant or bar, usually one he owns. He's always got someone tailing him, and I just assumed it was because he had money, as you can never be too careful these days. Now, I'm wondering if he needs protection because he's running in bad circles. *Just like Fury.*

He offers a small smile as I grab a bottle of Jack and pour us each one. "You really didn't need to come and see me."

He takes the glass and sips it. "If you're gonna break things off, at least look me in the eye."

I'm confused by his choice of words and give a small laugh. "Donnie, we've been on a handful of dates. It's not like I'm breaking off an engagement."

"I'm gonna lay my cards on the table, Xanthe," he says firmly, taking a seat at the table and gesturing for me to do the same. "I like you. A lot."

"You hardly know me."

"Don't do that," he says on a sigh. "Don't play down our feelings. You're upset because of tonight. You saw a different side to my world and it scared you. But I am exactly who you've been on dates with. That is me. This other side, the darker side, it's one you won't see again."

"But it's still there," I point out. "Who was that kid?"

He takes another drink. "My son."

"What?" I gasp. It doesn't matter he has a son, but it matters he never mentioned it.

"I didn't say anything because he doesn't really have much to do with me. His mum hates me, and occasionally, he pops up out the blue like he did tonight. Usually when he needs help."

"How old is he?"

"Sixteen." I arch a surprised brow. "We had him young. I was eighteen, and his mum was sixteen. We weren't together."

"Why didn't you tell me?"

"Because it didn't come up. I want to be honest now so we can make this work."

I'm already shaking my head as I stand and begin to pace. "It won't work."

"Before tonight, it worked."

"Before tonight, I just thought you were some rich guy with a good job."

"I am."

"What's your job?" I ask, fixing him with a glare.

He smirks. "I'm an entrepreneur."

"A criminal," I snap.

He stands abruptly, and for a second, I think he's going to grab me, but instead, he takes a deep breath. "No, Xanthe. I'm a businessman with a lot of fingers in a lot of pies." He takes my hand, and when I don't pull back, he gently tugs me against him and wraps his strong arms around me. I rest my head against his chest and inhale his spicy aftershave. It's one of the things that first attracted me to him.

He strokes a hand down my hair and tips my head back until we're staring at one another. "One chance," he whispers before kissing me. It's not our first kiss, but each one makes my toes curl and my insides melt. "I swear, I won't let you down again."

∼

I WAKE TO THE SOUND OF MY MOBILE RINGING. I GLANCE AT Donnie, who's sleeping deeply beside me, and snatch it up, cancelling the call from Fury before sliding out of bed and grabbing his shirt. I pull it on and head out the room, gently closing the door behind me.

I go into the kitchen and press call, and he answers straight away. "Are you okay?"

"Yes," I hiss.

"I've been texting you, Xanth. I've been going out my mind with worry."

"Well, you can relax. I'm fine."

"Did he take it well?"

"Yeah," I lie, wincing.

"Great. Open the door, I'm outside."

"What?" I gasp, my eyes widening. "Why?"

"Because I was worried."

CHAPTER 4

Fury

Xanthe opens the door, and I smile with relief. "Thank fuck. You have no idea how close I was to kicking your door in."

I frown as she steps out onto the path, closing the door behind her. She's acting odd, like she doesn't want me here, and then I allow my eyes to take in the shirt she's wearing. It's a man's shirt. "Well, as you can see, I'm fine," she says, sounding breezy yet panicked.

I pull the shirt up slightly, and she bats my hands away. "Naked," I note. "It's a man's shirt. Jesus, Xanth, tell me he's not still in there."

"We talked," she whispers, staring at the ground.

"Oh my god, he's in there, asleep in your fucking bed?" Her mouth opens and closes a few times before she nods. "What happened to breaking it off?" I hiss.

"We're taking it slow, and we're not exclusive or anything."

I'm already backing down the path. "You'll regret it."

"I might not."

"I know him, Xanthe. I know some of his dirty secrets, and I'm telling you, this is a mistake."

"I can walk away at any time," she argues.

I scoff, shaking my head in amusement. "If you believe that, you're a bigger idiot than I thought."

∼

I HIT THE GYM HARD. THERE'S NO WAY I CAN SLEEP RIGHT NOW while I'm so angry. Not now I know she's with him. Of all the men in the fucking world, how the hell did she end up with him?

I get back to the club two hours later and manage to sleep for a few hours before sunrise, and then I hit the gym again before heading to Donnie's place, surprised when I find him there. He looks happy, which pisses me off further. "I was thinking of moving your boxing match to one of my better clubs," he tells me.

"Why?"

"Because I'd like to make it more of an event rather than an underground match. I can make much more on the betting side of things if I hold a legit match. I'll invite some of my bigger clients, but be warned, there will be all members of society there, including police officers."

"I don't think your bent coppers will care where the match is as long as they get to see some blood."

He arches a brow. "You know, if you play nice, I will reward you very well."

I scoff. "I just wanna pay this debt off and be on my way."

He grins. "Take the day to rest or work out or whatever you fighters do. I don't need you. I have a hot date."

"With the nurse?" I ask.

He grins wider. "Yes. She's falling for my charm."

"I didn't think a guy like you would want to be tied down."

"What can I say, she turned my head," he says, winking before heading off into his office.

Chevy is leaning in the kitchen doorway. "He's got it bad."

"Seems so," I mutter.

"He's got big hopes for you at the fight tonight," he adds. "Don't let him down." And then he goes back into the kitchen.

I head back to the clubhouse, stopping by Axel's office. "Where the fuck have you been?" he demands.

"Donnie," I say as way of explanation.

"Oh yeah, what's he up to?"

I shrug. "Not much. He's moving the fight from the underground club to a legitimate setting."

"Why?"

"Reckons he'll make more money that way seeing as he's not fixing it."

"Do you know who you're fighting?" he asks.

I shake my head. "I don't care. I'll beat him."

He laughs. "That's what I like to hear."

∼

THE CLUB DONNIE IS USING FOR THE MATCH IS UPMARKET. WAY better than any place I've ever fought in before. Even the changing rooms are kitted out well.

Axel holds up the pads, and I punch them in turn, moving quickly as he backs away. The door opens, and Donnie comes in with Xanthe on his arm. I run my eyes over the shimmering white dress clinging to her curves and diamonds hanging from her ears, and I roll my eyes. It didn't take him long to have her looking the part.

"Are you ready?" he asks, shaking hands with Axel and Grizz.

"Yep," I mutter, turning to the punch bag instead.

Donnie steps away with Axel, and Xanthe stands awkwardly watching me. "Good luck," she murmurs.

"Thanks."

"Look," she whispers, moving a step closer. "I'm fine. Honestly."

"Good," I mutter, hitting the bag harder.

"I don't want us to fight about it."

"I don't even know you anymore," I say, frowning in irritation. "I don't care what you do or who you date." I know my words hurt her because her face displays it well as she steps back and heads towards the door.

"Xanthe," says Donnie, looking concerned.

"I need some air," she tells him, and he places a gentle kiss on her forehead.

"I'll come with you."

Once they've gone, Grizz holds the bag still for me to hit. "What was that about?"

"Nothing."

"Didn't look like nothing."

"I used to know Xanthe," I admit. "But Donnie doesn't know that."

"And you've met up again through him?" he asks.

"No. She was the nurse who treated me after Donnie's men laid into me."

"Fuck. It's a small world. She mean anything to you?"

I shake my head. "Nope."

Fletch opens the door. "They're ready for you," he calls to me.

Axel hits me on the back. "Good luck, brother."

We walk out to the ring together, my brothers behind me. A few people cheer, but most are too busy getting last-minute bets in. I climb into the ring and glance around while Axel removes my robe. I spot Xanthe in the front row with a few female friends. Donnie is at the next table with men I don't know. He tips his head my way, a warning that I am expected to win.

I jump about and stretch my legs while the other boxer gets into the ring. He's big, bigger than me, and I haven't seen him before, which is concerning seeing as I've been working the circuit hard these last few weeks and have met most heavyweights in my league.

Axel leans close to my ear as he shoves my mouth guard in. "I wouldn't put it past Donnie to have fixed this so you lose," he whispers. "Don't give him the satisfaction."

The referee calls us to the middle and tells us the usual rules. Then he wipes our gloves down his shirt before signalling for us to go to our corners. The bell rings, and my mind focusses in on the beast opposite me. His footing is off, and he's holding his left arm closer to his body like he's in pain. As I get closer, I see faint bruising under his eyes, which means he's fought recently, like me.

My first punch lands on his left side, right to the ribs, and he winces. I follow it quickly with two more punches, and he stumbles back. "Fuck me," I mutter, "are you even a boxer?"

He dashes a fist towards my head, and I dodge it, ducking down and hitting him in the ribs again. He almost doubles over, and I land a couple to his head. I back him to the ropes, caging him in the corner and hitting him continuously. The crowd is loud, cheering my name as I lay into him. I glance at Xanthe, who is yelling too, making me smile. And then the bell rings, and I head back to my corner.

Xanthe

"I thought you hated violence," says Jorja, laughing as I lower back into my seat.

I laugh too. "I don't know what came over me."

"Bloodlust," says Julianna. "It sends women into a frenzy."

"Especially when the guy fighting looks as good as that," adds Jorja.

I glance over to Donnie's table to make sure he's not listening. "Remember what I said," I whisper.

"Relax, he's not paying any attention," says Julianna. "How much of a coincidence is that?" she asks. "Your ex working for your new man."

"He isn't my new man," I say, rolling my eyes. "And can I class Fury as an ex? We were teenagers."

"How old exactly?" asks Jorja.

I shrug. "Fourteen until we were about sixteen."

"Two years?" she hisses, her eyes wide with surprise.

"We weren't actually fooling around until we were fifteen, so maybe nine months at a push," I argue. "And again, we were just kids."

"You had sex," says Jorja. "You were together."

"It doesn't matter anyway," I say dismissively. "He's not how I remember him."

"Was he always so fit?" asks Julianna.

I watch the way Fury moves around the ring with grace, despite him being over six-foot and well-built. "He always loved to fight," I say wistfully, remembering how he'd train hard in the local gym with some old guy who'd boxed for years. "It was the only time he was happy."

"But I bet he didn't always look like that," says Jorja, grinning.

I take in the tattoos crawling over his thick muscles, loving the way his skin glistens under the lights. He always had a good body, but nothing compared to how he is now. "Donnie has a good body too," I point out.

"Hey, we're not comparing," says Jorja innocently.

"All I'm saying is if there was a dark room and I was stuck

between those two, I know I'd climb that huge fucker first," adds Julianna, and both girls burst into laughter.

I roll my eyes, shaking my head with amusement.

There're huge cheers from the crowd as Fury hits his opponent hard in the face, causing him to fall against the ropes. The referee gets between them, waving his arms, and Fury grins, holding both arms in the air. "What's happening?" I ask.

"Your man just won," says Jorja.

"He's not my man," I hiss.

"Good, cos if there's an after-party, I fully intend to talk to him."

~

Donnie slips his hand into mine while I'm patiently waiting at the bar. "Are you enjoying the evening?" he asks.

"Very much," I say with a smile. "Thank you."

"Your friends wasted no time introducing themselves to my boxer," he says, nodding to where Fury has just stepped into the room freshly showered and is now chatting with Jorja and Julianna.

"They have no decorum," I joke, forcing a smile, but inside, I feel a pang of jealousy.

"Let me introduce you properly," he adds, leading me towards them before I can refuse.

"I met him already," I say, pulling back a little.

"Not officially," says Donnie. "Well done," he says to Fury and holds his hand out. Fury eyes it with contempt before taking it. "You did well. I see you've met Xanthe's friends, so I thought I'd introduce you to Xanthe officially," he says, smiling back at me. "Xanthe, this is Fury. Fury, this is Xanthe."

Fury holds out his hand, and I take it, ignoring the spark

of electricity shooting up my arm at our contact. "Nice to meet you properly," I mutter. "Well done."

"You should get your eye checked again," says Donnie, and I glance up to see the old cut above Fury's eye has split open again, leaking blood down his face.

"Oh, leave it. It adds to the effect," says Jorja with a flirtatious smile.

"I can seal it," I offer, the words tumbling out before I can stop them.

Donnie glances back, frowning. "Are you sure?"

"Of course."

"I'm fine," says Fury. "It's just a scratch."

"That is bleeding down your face," says Donnie stiffly. "Xanthe will look at it for you."

I don't miss the way Fury rolls his eyes in irritation before turning back towards the door he just came from. I follow, struggling to keep up as he marches ahead and into another room.

He grabs a first aid kit and practically throws it in my direction. I catch it, watching cautiously as he sits down. "There should be glue in there," he mutters.

I place the kit on the bench beside him and open it, taking out a piece a gauze to wipe the cut. I hold the back of his head and press it, applying pressure to try to stop the bleeding. "Why are you mad at me?" I eventually ask.

"I'm not mad."

"I know you," I remind him, and he scoffs. "I know you," I repeat more firmly, "and I know when you're pissed."

"Why him?" he snaps, pushing to his feet and towering over me. The gauze drops to the floor as my hand falls away from his face. "All the fucking men in London and you choose him? When you weren't here, I could forget about you and pretend you were leading a good life," he continues, anger radiating from him. "You were married with kids and a dog. You had a nice house," he snaps, tapping his head, "in here."

"I'm happy," I whisper.

"But now, I can see that none of that is true and you're still coasting along in life, still fucking scumbags," he snaps. "Still making the wrong choices."

"You're one to talk," I mutter.

"I never stood a chance, Xanth. My life was set to this, but yours wasn't."

"Which one were you, Reese, a scumbag or a wrong choice?"

"Fury," he bellows. "My fucking name is Fury." I can't stop the tears as they balance carelessly on my lower lash line. "I was a wrong choice," he hisses, "but you insisted on pursuing it, and where did that leave me, Xanth? On the first train outta there."

I inhale sharply at his words. "You blame me?" I gasp. "They found you a permanent foster home."

"They found out I was fucking their daughter," he cries angrily, stepping back and gripping handfuls of his hair. "I was good enough to foster but not to be with their little girl."

My mouth falls open, hardly believing his words. "No," I whisper. "They found a couple who were looking to adopt a teenage boy."

"When does that ever happen?" he yells. "You know the statistics—no one gets adopted in their teens, especially not a teenage boy." I feel my cheeks burn with embarrassment. I believed my parents when they sat me down and told me the social worker had found him a new home. "You believed what you wanted to believe," he almost whispers.

"I didn't know," I mutter.

The door opens, and Chevy sticks his head in. "Everything okay? What's taking so long?"

I immediately turn away and busy myself looking through

the first aid bag. "I feel sick," says Fury. "She thinks I have a concussion. I was just telling her I'm good to go."

"You should rest," I cut in to keep up the act.

"Just glue the eye and get back out there. Boss is getting irritated," he mutters, leaving again.

Fury sits on the bench and tips his head back, closing his eyes. I pinch his cut together and squeeze the glue across it. Being so close to him suddenly feels too much, and when he trails a hand up the back of my leg, resting it against my backside, I inhale sharply. "I missed you," he whispers. "I told myself that staying away was for the best, but now, I'm not so sure." He opens his eyes, and we stare at one another. "If you're going to date a prick, then at least choose me."

I step back, and his hand falls away. "You don't mean that," I whisper.

"Every. Single. Word."

The door opens, and Donnie storms in. "What's going on?"

I drop the glue in the bag and zip it closed, turning to smile at Donnie. "Your fighter is stubborn," I say, my tone teasing. "He should rest. He's concussed."

"He'll be fine," mutters Donnie, grabbing my hand. "There are people I want you to meet." And he practically marches me out of there.

CHAPTER 5

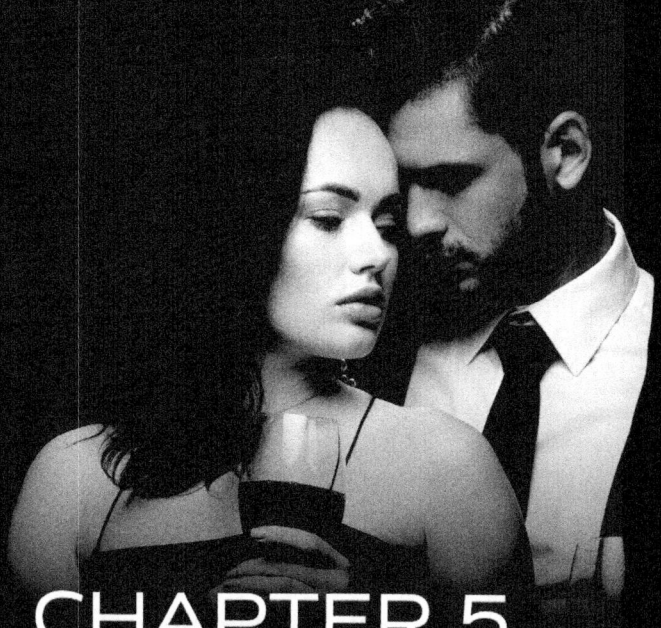

Fury

I knock back the whiskey Axel hands me and wince. I'm starting to feel pain in my jaw, and my ribs still hurt from the previous fight. "You should be happy," says Grizz. "He paid you for tonight even though you owe him."

"He paid me because he wants me to owe him," I snap. "I told him to keep my cut, but he wouldn't."

"Maybe he likes having you around," says Axel with a grin.

"I can't think why," says Fletch, his voice dripping with sarcasm.

"I told her to walk away," I mutter, fixing my eyes on Xanthe as she and Donnie move around the room together hand-in-hand. "And instead, she slept with him."

Axel follows my glare. "The nurse?"

"Why would you tell her to walk away?" asks Fletch. He's my closest brother seeing as we were in the Nottingham charter together for a time.

"That's Xanthe," I tell him, and his eyes widen in surprise.

"Fuck, brother. And she's dating Donnie?" I nod. "I mean, she's stunning. I can see why you'd be pissed."

"Someone gonna fill me in?" asks Grizz.

"He had a thing with her when he was a teenager," says Fletch.

"Ouch," says Grizz, patting me on the back. "Axel and Fletch can both sympathise with you there."

"I don't advise you get in the middle of whatever she's got going with Donnie," warns Axel.

"He's right," agrees Grizz. "Sit back. He'll soon get bored. He never stays with one woman for long."

"Put your attention elsewhere," adds Fletch. "You have a fan club right there."

He nods towards where Xanthe's friends are sitting, occasionally glancing my way. "Let's go charm them," adds Grizz, pushing me towards them.

"Ladies," I greet, "can I get you a drink?"

One of the women points to the bottle of Champagne on the table. "Donnie sorted it," she says.

"Of course, he did," I mutter.

"I'm Grizz," he says, holding out a hand and shaking each of theirs.

"I'm Julianna. I work with Xanthe. And this is Jorja, her best friend."

I sit beside Jorja. Grizz makes an excuse about needing to speak to Axel and rushes off, leaving us alone. "So," says Jorja, "you love my bestie."

I frown. "I don't even know her."

"Bullshit, I can tell by your face. You haven't stopped searching the room for her."

"I'm worried about her," I admit. "Donnie Nelson is bad news."

They both lean closer. "In what way?" asks Julianna.

"In every possible bad way you can think of," I reply. "He's not the sort of man she should be with."

"Is that coming from a jealous ex or a concerned friend?" asks Jorja.

"Both," I admit.

They exchange a worried look. "Okay, we'll talk to her," says Julianna. "Give Jorja your number, and she'll let you know what she says."

Jorja hands me her mobile, and I input my number right as Xanthe joins us. She arches a brow as she slides in beside Julianna. "Having a good night?" she asks.

"Great," Jorja replies. "You?"

"I've had better," she mutters as I hand the mobile back. "We should head home. We have a shift tomorrow," she says to Julianna.

"You need me to drive?" I ask as they stand.

"Chevy is taking us," she says coldly before wandering off.

"I'll call," whispers Jorja, rushing after her.

∽

I GET HOME TWO HOURS LATER TO FIND JENNIE IN MY BED sleeping. I groan, turning and heading right back out.

I pull out my mobile and see a message from Xanthe left over an hour ago.

> Xanthe: I need to see you.

> Me: Are you still awake?

> Xanthe: Yes.

> Me: On my way.

I arrive within five minutes but park my bike a street away, just in case Donnie happens to drive past.

I raise my fist to knock right as she yanks the door open. She heads into the kitchen, leaving me to follow.

She sits at the table, pulling her dressing gown tightly around herself. "Sit," she mutters, pointing to the chair opposite hers. I lower into it, and she fixes me with a glare. "You told my friends to have a chat with me," she accuses.

"That's not what I said," I argue, shifting uncomfortably. "I told them he was bad news, which he is."

"I'm a grown woman, Fury. I can do what I like." She sighs heavily. "I didn't ask you here to talk about that. I want to know what happened when we were kids."

I groan. "What's the point?"

"Tell me everything."

"Why? It'll only hurt you more, and you'll feel betrayed."

"By you or my parents?" she asks.

"Your parents," I mutter.

"I need to know, Fury, because I've spent years ignoring the twist in my heart whenever I think about you, which is actually way more than I'd like it to be."

I try not to smile at her confession. "Your dad caught me in your bed," I tell her, and her eyes widen. "He gently tapped me on the shoulder to wake me, and I'll never forget the disappointed look in his eyes as he pointed to the door. I crept from your bed, leaving you to sleep blissfully unaware, and I went downstairs, where he and your mum were waiting for me. Turns out they'd suspected for days, and your mum had heard us that night." I notice her cheeks burn red with embarrassment. "They gave me the talk about how you were going places," I say, running my finger over the scratch on her oak table. "And that by dating me, those chances would be ruined. I tried to tell them . . . I tried to fight for us," I explain, offering a small smile, "but they weren't interested. They said we couldn't be in love, that we were too young to know what that was."

"I had no idea," she mutters. "I was trying to remember back to that day. I woke, and they were acting so normal."

"They'd already called the social worker and said if I left quietly, they wouldn't pursue charges of underage sex and grooming."

"Grooming?" she repeats, looking horrified.

"I was two years older, Xanth. We started having sex when you were fifteen. They found your diary."

"Oh shit," she hisses. "I'd kept track of every sexual encounter in there." She buries her face in her hands.

"They had evidence. And let's face it, a foster kid having sex with the foster carer's daughter, a judge would've slapped a charge on me, no questions."

She slides her face up, keeping her hands over her mouth. "I am so sorry," she mutters.

"It was easier to just leave."

"You could've written to me," she says.

"How? What if your parents intercepted the letters? They would've had me arrested, Xanth. I gratefully took the clean slate, but the terms were that I stay clear of you."

"I was so heartbroken," she admits, tears making her eyes glisten. "They just told me you'd been moved to another home where a couple were looking to adopt. I forced myself to be happy for you because you needed a good family, but deep down, I was in bits."

I take a breath, thankful we're finally having this conversation because fuck knows I need to get it off my chest. "I was angry," I admit. "For letting you talk me into it. I'd been happy with your parents, and I hated that I'd been sent away, rejected again. I spent years being angry at you." The words tumble out, even though I don't mean them to.

Her expression fills with guilt, making me feel bad, but it's the truth, and she needs to know it all. "I don't blame you," she mutters. "I'm so sorry."

I stand and round the table, crouching in front of her. I take her hands and stare as our fingers entwine. "It wasn't your fault. It was just easier to blame you. Truth is, even if you hadn't convinced me, we would've ended up together. I loved you so much."

Xanthe cups my face in her hands. "I loved you too," she tells me with a watery smile.

We stare at one another for a few seconds. I sense she's about to kiss me, and deep down, I know I should stop her, but my body refuses to move. I feel the warmth of her breath across my face, and then she gently presses her lips to mine. It's wary and cautious. My mind takes me back to how things were, and suddenly, we're right back in her room, sneaking around.

I stand, taking her with me and sliding my hands into her hair, gripping it at the base and losing myself in the kiss. My cock is pushing against her stomach, and she lifts herself onto the table, sliding back while pulling my belt open. She reaches into my jeans, her hand gripping my erection, freeing it from my boxers. I loosen the cord on her dressing gown and push it from her shoulders, gliding my hands down her naked body.

I step back slightly, taking in her perfect curves. We lock eyes, both panting for breath, and then I close the gap again, trailing kisses along her jaw while she clings to my shoulders. I pepper them along her collar bone and down her chest, stopping at her pebbled nipple. *Fuck, she's as perfect as I remember.* I circle it with my tongue, enjoying the sound as she inhales sharply.

"Condom?" she pants.

I feel for my wallet, retrieving a condom, and she takes it from me, ripping it open with her teeth. She takes it from the packet, discarding the foil and pinching the end of the rubber before expertly pushing it onto my cock. I hiss at the contact as she sheaths me, itching to slow it down so I can savour every second but also desperate to be inside of her.

"You sure about this?" I ask, trailing more kisses along her collar bone. She wraps her legs around me and tugs me closer, pressing my erection against her opening. It's all the confirmation I need, sliding into her and groaning in pleasure as she grips my cock tightly.

Her arms wrap around my neck, and she pulls me in for another kiss as I slowly fuck her, taking my time to feel every inch of her. *Fuck knows I've thought about it for long enough.*

She was my first, and at sixteen years old, I couldn't get enough of her. She was wild and horny all the time, and we'd spend hours exploring each other. Those memories are burned into my brain.

I feel her hand between us, rubbing herself, but I bat it away and take over, pressing my thumb to her swollen clit with just enough pressure to have her on the edge. She squirms beneath me, whimpering each time I slow down. I pull from her, and she groans in frustration, but as I kiss down her body and rest between her legs, she props herself up on her elbows, watching as I run my tongue through her folds. She bites on her lower lip in that sexy way I love, her eyes full of heat. Her fingers run through my hair, gently gripping it as I work her into a frenzy. And right before she's about to come, I stand and slam back into her, fucking her hard.

She cries out, her nails digging into my shoulders as I chase my own release. I feel the wetness between us as she squirts, and it's enough to drag my orgasm from me, causing me to shudder uncontrollably as I empty into the condom. "Fuck," I pant, closing my eyes as I try to slow my rapid breaths.

I pull from her and grab a tea towel from beside us, wiping her arousal from the worktop and then pressing it between her legs. She lies lifeless, her hands above her head in all her naked glory for me to appreciate.

I press gentle kisses along her inner thigh, occasionally nipping the skin. "That was . . . unexpected."

Xanthe

S*HIT. SHIT. SHIT.* I push to sit up, and Fury's hopeful face stares back at me. I slip off the counter, and he stands, trapping me between him and the worktop. He slides a hand along my jaw, tipping my head back slightly to make eye contact. "Are you okay?"

I nod, forcing a smile. "I need the bathroom."

"Xanth," he whispers, his expression full of concern.

"I'm fine," I say a little too sharply as I move past him, slipping my mobile from the counter discreetly. "Honestly."

The second I get into the bathroom, I turn the tap on full and groan out loud. "Fuck." I take a deep breath, and then I call Jorja, my go-to whenever I fuck up.

"Huh?" she answers, sounding sleepy.

"It's me," I whisper.

"Are you in the shower?"

"No, listen, I fucked up."

"Again?" I hear rustling like she's sitting up. "Jesus, what time is it?"

"I slept with the fighter."

"Oh, you lucky bitch."

"Jorja, I slept with him after sleeping with Donnie a few nights ago. I'm literally a whore."

"A single whore," she says on a yawn.

"I don't think Donnie will see it like that."

She sighs heavily. "Look, have you actually said the words out loud to either of them? Have any of you established any kind of relationship?"

"No, but I'm the kind of girl who expects a man to be one hundred percent faithful once I've had sex with him. I'm a hypocrite."

"If no one said the words, you're all good."

I scrub my hand over my face. "What do I do now?"

"Enjoy the rest of the night with the fighter."

"I can't do that, Jorja," I say, groaning.

"Why the hell not? If you're gonna waste a perfectly good man, send him my way."

"Can we just be serious for one minute?" I snap.

"Which one do you like the most?"

"We're not in primary school," I argue.

"It all comes down to who you like the most, Xanth. Pros and cons to eliminate the loser."

"It's not as simple as that. I have a history with Reese. Unfinished business."

"And Donnie?"

"He's a gentleman. Kind. He paid for our entire night and insisted I invite you guys to join us."

"He is rich," she adds. "What's the fighter's bank balance like?"

"I have no idea," I snap, "and it's not about money."

"Okay, who was the best in bed?"

I groan louder. "I'm disconnecting now," I singsong, ending the call.

I brace my hands against the sink and stare at myself in the mirror. "Get it together, you slag," I whisper. "You've done it now. It's how you handle it from here."

I go to my room and pull on a set of pyjamas before heading back downstairs where Donnie is standing by the worktop. I stare wide-eyed, glancing around for a sign that Fury is still here. He smiles wide. "I called up to you, but it sounded like the shower was running."

The lump in my throat threatens to choke me as I try to form a sentence. "How did you . . . erm, how did you get in?"

"The front door," he says, smirking. "Like I said, I called up to you, but you didn't hear me. You should have that locked at all times, baby. Who knows who'll walk in."

"Right," I mutter, nodding. "Drink?" He nods.

I spot the two glasses on the worktop and immediately throw a tea towel over them, realising it's the towel Fury used to clean up the mess we made. I glance back to where Donnie is sitting, his arms resting on the worktop I haven't yet cleaned properly. I wince, feeling mortified.

I grab two new glasses and pour whiskey into both, knocking mine back in one and topping up again.

I hand Donnie his glass, and his free hand glides around my waist. He tugs me to stand between him and the counter, just like Fury did moments ago. "Thank you for coming tonight. I loved having you there."

"Thanks for inviting me," I squeak, knocking the second drink back.

He places his whiskey down and runs his hands over my shoulders. "I missed having you to myself." He nuzzles into my neck, and I feel his erection pressing against me.

"Donnie, listen," I mutter. His kisses continue down my neck, and his hands now grip my backside, pulling me against him. "Please," I whisper, pressing my hands to his chest and applying a gentle amount of pressure to make him stop.

"Baby, all I've thought about all evening is you in that dress and . . ." He catches my mouth, kissing me.

I'm almost lost to him when an image of Fury enters my head, and I slam my hands against him and push him to step back. "Stop," I snap.

He stares wide-eyed. "What's wrong?"

"We need to talk."

"You look serious," he notes, his smile fading.

"I feel like we're moving a bit fast," I begin, shifting uncomfortably.

"Too fast?"

I nod. "Yeah, you can't just turn up here, Donnie."

"You're upset because I let myself in?"

"You took me by surprise."

His eyes narrow. "Wait, do you have another man here?"

I shake my head, my eyes widening in panic. "No. No. Of course not."

His eyes are blazing with what I think is anger . . . or jealousy. He takes off before my mind can catch up, heading for the living room. I race after him. My heart leaps into my throat because I have no idea where Fury is or if he's still in the house. I try to grab Donnie's arm, and he shrugs me off, causing me to stumble back. "I'll fucking kill him," he bellows.

"Donnie, stop," I cry as he scans the living room before taking the stairs two at a time. I run after him. "Donnie, this is crazy."

He slams each door back against the wall with force as he checks the rooms. When he gets to my room, he pauses, holding on to the door handle. "Last chance," he warns me. "Tell me who he is."

"There's no one," I yell, hardly believing the way he's reacting right now.

He grabs my upper arm as he shoves the door open. I breathe a sigh of relief when I see it's empty. Donnie pulls me into the room, glancing around like a maniac. "Was someone here?" he growls.

"No," I whisper. I don't like the look in his eyes as he pierces me, trying to work out if I'm lying. "You're hurting me," I add, and his eyes fall to where he's gripping me hard. He releases me instantly, like he's only just realised, and takes a step back.

"Shit. Fuck. I'm sorry," he says desperately. "I'm so sorry."

"You should go," I mutter, wrapping my arms around myself. I feel sick from the adrenaline currently coursing through my body. I'm not cut out for this type of confrontation.

He suddenly places his hands on my upper arms, and I flinch. There's remorse in his expression as he gently runs them up and down my arms. "Baby, I am so sorry. I just . . ." He turns his back and runs his hands through his hair. "I send myself crazy with jealousy." He turns back to me, and I think I see the glistening of tears in his eyes. "I really like you, Xanthe. The thought of you with another man sends me nuts."

"We're not together," I say firmly, and that dangerous glint returns to his eyes, but he shuts it down fast. "We never said we were exclusive. You don't own me."

"I know," he says, holding up his hands in an appeasing manner. "I'm out of order and totally jumping the gun. But I like you, what can I say?" He shrugs helplessly.

"I won't be with someone who lays a hand on me."

"Baby, I'd never hurt you."

"You just did," I snap. "Please go." I'm aware that I'm alone in my bedroom with a man who has the potential to lose his shit again, so I soften my features and add, "We'll talk tomorrow when we've both slept on it."

"I can't leave you like this," he says, shrugging from his jacket.

My heart slams faster in my chest. "I want to be alone."

"I won't lay a finger on you, I swear," he promises, kicking his shoes off. "Let's sleep on it, and tomorrow, we can forget it ever happened."

"I don't want to forget it," I say, frowning. "Please just go."

"You're angry, I get it, but we can't sort shit out if I'm not here with you." He continues to undress, and I fight back my tears. "Baby, we've had our first argument. It's normal. Don't look so sad."

"I'd like to be on my own," I repeat.

He shakes his head, a big smile on his face. "I can't allow it, Xanth. My mother always said you should never leave on an argument. Now, put this on." He holds out his shirt for me.

"I'm fine in my pyjamas," I mutter.

"Xanth," he says, that smile still slapped on his face but with a dangerous glint, "put it on."

I feel tears building, and I try to swallow them down. "I'll sleep in the spare room tonight," I mutter, backing towards the door.

He grins, slamming his hand against it so I can't open it. I jump with fright. "Nuh-uh. We sleep in the same bed until this is sorted."

I inhale sharply, desperately trying to stay calm. "I need space."

"You need to be with me, so we can talk when you're ready." He moves closer, gently kissing me on the forehead. He's not being threatening, yet I feel terrified just by his demeanour. He unbuttons my pyjama top, slipping it from me and replacing it with his shirt. "Shorts too," he whispers against my cheek. Tears leak from my eyes as I push my shorts down, too scared to deny him. "Good girl." His praise only sickens me further.

He leads me to the bed, pulling back the covers and patting the mattress. I climb in, a million thoughts racing through my head as he rounds the bed and climbs in the other side in just his boxers. He tugs me into his side, holding me against him while calmly stroking my hair. I swipe a stray tear from my cheek. "Don't get upset," he whispers. "It was just an argument." The fact he's playing down what just happened screams red flag.

Fuck. I should have listened to Fury.

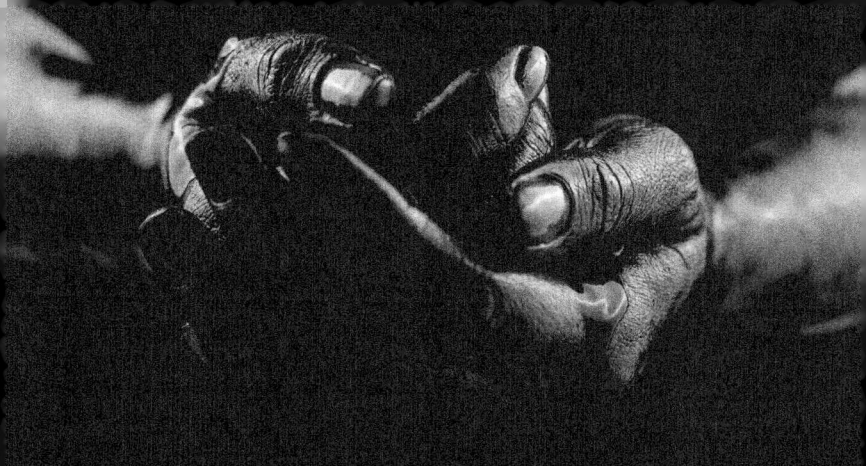

CHAPTER 6

Fury

"What's up with your face?" asks Nyx, sitting beside me at the kitchen table.

I stare at the text message from Donnie. I'm gripping my phone so tight, the tips of my fingers are white. "I've gotta pick Donnie up," I reply.

"It's shit you gotta work for him like this," says Nyx, piling bacon onto his plate. "You've done well not to smack him in the face."

"Just biding my time," I mutter bitterly.

"Don't do anything to piss Pres off," says Grizz. "You did right getting outta there last night. If he'd have caught you with his woman, you'd both be dead now."

"She ain't his woman," I spit.

"She ain't yours either," he reminds me. "And until this shit with Donnie is done, you need to stay clear. It'll cause nothing but trouble."

The second I heard Donnie shout her name last night, I

dashed out the back door. But knowing he spent the night there pisses me off. Grizz pats me on the shoulder. "Look, she's probably dumped him. Don't read too much into that text. He could've turned up there again this morning, for all you know."

I nod, standing. "Yeah, probably."

I ARRIVE AT XANTHE'S AND KNOCK LIGHTLY ON THE DOOR. Donnie opens it looking freshly showered in a clean suit. "Xanthe," he calls, "I'm leaving now."

She appears in the kitchen doorway, and I ball my fists at my sides at seeing her in his shirt. Donnie turns, going to her, and as he embraces her, our eyes connect. Hers are full of regret, and mine probably match my mood . . . angry.

"I'll wait in the car," I mutter, spinning on my heel and forcing myself back up the garden path.

I'm waiting a few minutes before Donnie slides into the back seat. "Where to?" I ask, keeping my eyes on the road ahead.

"The fight club," he replies, pulling out his mobile. He presses it to his ear as I pull out and head for the club. "Good morning. I'd like to send the biggest bouquet of white roses you can find," he says into the mobile. "Put them on my account. Mister Donnie Nelson." I hate that name, and my hands curl tighter around the steering wheel. "Yes, add a note," he continues. "My everything," he adds, and I almost roll my eyes. "Forgive me." He waits a beat before thanking them and disconnecting. "Women," he says, catching my eye in the rearview mirror. "They're so easily upset."

"I wouldn't know," I mutter.

He arches a brow. "You've never upset a woman?" He looks amused.

"No. I try not to."

"We all try," he says, "but sometimes we slip up. But it's fine, she's forgiven me." I inhale sharply, trying to keep my cool. "Would you go back for her and drive her to the hospital?" he asks.

It's the first time I haven't wanted to see her since I first bumped into her. "Sure thing."

"She'll protest. Don't take no for an answer." I stop outside his club, and he opens the door. "Oh, and Fury, let me know if she texts or calls anyone."

I frown. "Do you want me to ask her who she's texting?"

"No. Just observe. Does she look happy texting whoever it is? Is she speaking to a man if she accepts a call?"

I give a stiff nod. "Got it."

I return to Xanthe's house and stare at the closed door. By having sex, I've opened myself up to her again. Now, I have to face the music.

I get out the car just as her door opens and she steps out. She doesn't see me right away and walks up the path with her head down, like she's lost in thought. It's only when I open the back door that she startles, and then that guilty expression returns. "Get in," I order.

She looks down the street. "I think I want to walk today."

"Not an option," I say firmly.

"Is that an order from him or you?"

I don't meet her eye, and she sighs heavily, getting into the car. I slam the door and get in the driver's seat. I start the engine as she puts her seatbelt on. "It wasn't what it looked like," she begins.

"I don't want to know," I spit.

"We didn't have sex," she adds.

I slam my hand against the steering wheel. "Stop talking," I yell, looking at her through the mirror. She presses her lips into a fine line. "I want to rip his head off," I hiss. "And if you tell me shit I can't handle, I'll kill him and then my President will kill me, so stop fucking talking."

We drive the short journey to the hospital in silence, and when we arrive, I get out and open her door. I don't look at her as she slides from the vehicle, but she pauses, composing herself. "I tried to end it with him," she whispers. "You were right. He's not a nice man." And before I can respond, she heads off inside.

I stare after her, her words playing on my mind. Then my mobile rings, and I drag myself back into the car before answering.

"Did she call anyone?" asks Donnie.

"No," I confirm.

"Text?"

"No."

"Did she say anything?" he demands, reminding me of a lovesick schoolboy.

"No." I pause before adding, "She looked sad, though. Upset even."

"Careful," he almost whispers. "Paying too much close attention to my woman gets my back up." And then he disconnects.

I throw my phone onto the passenger seat and get back out the car, marching into the hospital. I see Xanthe by the nurse's station, and her eyes widen in surprise, but I don't give her a chance to speak before I grab her hand and pull her into a side room. Another nurse rushes after us. "I'll call security," she threatens.

"It's fine," says Xanthe, giving a reassuring smile. "I know him." The nurse reluctantly leaves. "You'll get me fired," she cries. And then she bursts into tears, burying her face in her hands. My anger instantly melts away, and I drag her into my arms, holding her against my chest and whispering words of comfort into her hair. When she calms, I tip her head back and wipe her tears with my thumbs. "I thought you were still in the house," she whimpers.

"I heard him come in," I admit. "I left through the back door."

"He searched the house," she whispers, wiping more tears on the sleeves of her cardigan. "He was so angry."

"He knows about us?"

She shakes her head. "He took me by surprise, and I was rattled. He guessed I'd had someone round and lost his mind." She cries some more. "And then he wouldn't leave."

"Did you ask him to?"

She shoves her hands against my chest, putting space between us. "Of course, I did."

"Sorry," I mutter, rubbing a hand over my forehead. "So, he just refused?"

"He's fucking mental," she hisses. "He was talking like we'd just had a little argument, insisting we'd be fine by the morning. I told him it wasn't going to work out, and he completely ignored me."

I stare at the floor, lost for words. I don't know what to tell her because Donnie never does anything he doesn't want to do. The more she protests, the more he'll push her. "I told you this would end badly," I mutter.

More sobs leave her. "Well, thanks, that really helps."

"You're gonna have to tell him about us."

Her eyes widen. "Are you mad?" she cries. "You didn't see him last night, Reese. He was crazy mad. He'll kill you and then me."

I cup her cheek. "I can handle myself, and he won't hurt you."

"I'm not risking it. The way he was talking . . ." She shudders. "He's not right in the head."

"So, now what?"

She shrugs. "I don't know. I'll ignore his calls, avoid him, and hope he gets bored."

I scoff. "He has you picked up for work and taken home.

He knows your shift pattern. He got into your house last night."

"The door was unlocked," she mutters.

"The door wasn't unlocked," I snap. "I locked it, Xanth. He got in anyway, and he'll continue to turn up unannounced."

Her body shakes with her crying, and she wraps her arms around herself. "I'll call the police."

"And say what? He'll twist it and make you look like the bad person. Plus, he's got people high up."

"So, I'm stuck with him?"

I sigh. "I'll think of something. Have you got somewhere else you can stay?"

"Not really. I don't want to drag anyone else into it."

"Leave early for work to avoid him. Send him a text message telling him it's over. Be clear. Then you have evidence you've told him, just in case by some miracle we can get some kind of restraining order."

"I'm scared," she whispers.

"He won't hurt you, Xanth. I'll kill him before that happens."

Xanthe

I FOLLOW FURY'S ADVICE, LEAVING WORK HALF AN HOUR EARLY. Instead of going straight home, I call Jorja and arrange to meet her for dinner.

The second she lays eyes on me, she's out of her chair and enveloping me in a hug. "What's wrong?"

We sit down, and with a sad smile, I say, "I can't cry anymore. My face is a mess."

"Didn't things go well with Donnie?"

I shake my head. "Fury was right—he's a nutter."

I fill her in, and she stares open-mouthed. "Oh my god,

what's wrong with him?"

"Fury said to try to avoid him, but how long can I do that for, realistically?"

"And why can't you just report him to the police?"

I shrug. "Fury reckons he's got people high up." I bury my face, groaning into my hands. "Who the hell is he anyway? I mean, people high up? What does that even mean?"

She smiles sympathetically. "You hear stories, don't you, about men like that? Maybe he's in some kind of mafia?"

I roll my eyes. "Don't be ridiculous."

"Well, how else do you explain it?"

I stare out the window. "I don't know. I need to send him a text, but I'm scared he'll be waiting for me at home."

"Stay at mine?"

I shake my head. "I don't want to drag anyone into it, especially if he is nuts."

"Okay, well, send the text now, and I'll drive past your house a few times to see if he's waiting."

I pull out my phone and type a text out.

> Me: I've spent the day thinking about last night. I've had a great time with you, but it's just not working out for me. I don't want to see you again. Please respect that.

I turn the phone to Jorja, and she nods, so I send it. "I feel sick," I mutter.

"Look, he's not the first nutter you've met, right? Men can be intimidating and crazy, but they soon get bored. Once he realises you're not entertaining him, he'll back off."

"I hope so," I say, but I have a bad feeling.

Once we've eaten dinner, Jorja drives me home. We slow outside, and I check the cars parked around the street, making sure they're empty. "I'll come in for a coffee," she says, parking up.

Inside, the place is dark, and I sigh with relief, turning on the lights. "Keep the bolt locked when you're home alone," she says, sliding it into place. "And the windows."

"Maybe Fury got it wrong," I say. "Maybe he didn't lock the door at all and just thought he did."

She nods. "Yeah, but still, lock up properly just in case."

"Jorja, do you think he'll get bored?"

She forces a smile, which I know confirms my own fears, but she nods. "Definitely."

∽

It's the middle of the night when I hear a distant banging. I open my eyes and check the clock, groaning when it reads two-thirty. The banging comes again, this time louder, and I sit up, frowning.

My heartrate doubles as I climb out of bed and pull the curtain back slightly so I can peek outside. Two men are holding another man up. He looks hurt, so I open my window. "What's going on?" I ask.

The two men look up, and I recognise one as Chevy. "He needs help," he tells me.

"No. Take him to a hospital," I snap.

"He won't make it," he yells. "Open the fucking door, now."

"No," I snap. "I'm not involved with your boss anymore, so find someone else."

"Don't you follow some code of practise?" he snaps.

"I'm not allowed to treat patients like this."

"Then make an exception, because if he dies, I'll tell the police you refused to help."

I growl in frustration and slam the window closed, grabbing my robe and rushing downstairs. I unlock the door, and they bustle in past me, heading straight for the kitchen. Chevy swipes the leftover mugs from the table, sending them crashing to the floor, then he helps his friend onto the surface.

"What happened?" I ask, lifting the man's shirt slightly to see blood.

"He got stabbed."

"Chevy, he might have serious internal bleeding. He needs a doctor."

"I have one coming, but until he gets here, you will keep him alive."

"It's not something I can promise," I snap, grabbing some scissors and cutting the man's T-shirt away. There's a deep wound to his side, and I gently press his stomach to feel for internal swelling that could indicate a bleed. "How much blood has he lost?"

"A lot," Chevy confirms.

I grab my first aid kit and pull out all the padded dressing, using them to apply pressure against the wound. "He'll probably need blood."

"The doctor's sorting that."

I frown. "How?"

"Don't worry your pretty little head." He stares down at his phone then heads to the back door, pulling it open. Fury enters, and the first thing I notice is that he's covered in blood. His jeans are soaked, and there are splatters on his shirt and face. He avoids my eyes, and before I can ask what the hell is going on, a doctor enters, filling me with relief.

Fury places a box down while the doctor places his bag on the table and retrieves some gloves. He proceeds to check the patient over. "We'll need to get inside," he states, looking at me.

"Huh?"

"It's possible the knife wound has perforated the liver."

I shake my head. "I'm not a scrub nurse," I say meekly. "He needs to go to hospital."

"I thought you said she was fine with all this?" the doctor snaps, glaring at Chevy.

Chevy grabs me by the upper arm and shoves me from

the room, closing the door. "Now, listen very carefully," he hisses. "You're going to go in there and help. I don't care what you have to do but do it."

"I can't," I cry. "I'll get into trouble."

"There's no choice," he snaps.

The door opens, and Fury looks back and forth between us. "Everything okay?"

"No," I say. "I can't do this."

He glances at Chevy. "Let me talk to her."

Chevy rolls his eyes in irritation and goes back into the kitchen. Fury closes the door. "What are you doing here?" I hiss. "Why are you covered in blood?"

"I'll explain later."

"I can't keep doing this, Reese. He can't keep sending people my way to be patched-up."

"Listen, until I figure a way out, you have to do this."

I scowl. "I don't have to do anything. I'm calling an ambulance and the police."

"That will land you in deeper waters. Plus . . ." he pauses, rubbing a hand over his forehead.

"What?" I growl, sensing it's not good news.

"He's going to keep using you. Chevy said he's got shit on you now, and he'll use that to make you do what he wants."

I stare wide-eyed. "What shit?"

"I don't know. Can you think of anything?"

I shake my head, fighting the tears that are threatening to fall again. "Why is he doing this to me?"

"I'm guessing his ego is bruised. I'll think of something." He presses a chaste kiss to my head before heading back into the kitchen, leaving me to follow.

CHAPTER 7

Fury

I wait patiently while Xanthe sews Logan's wound. He works security at the fight club, and things got out of hand tonight. There're always some fuckers thinking they can take on the world, and Logan is a big bastard, so it took a few of them to bring him to the ground, then they set on him like a pack of fucking animals. By the time we got there, they were gone, and he was bleeding out.

"Spare room?" asks Chevy, and Xanthe looks fit to burst.

"Absolutely not," she snaps.

"He needs bed rest," the doctor confirms, looking at her.

"This is my home," she yells.

"And he will need a nurse to keep an eye on him for the next few hours," the doctor continues.

"Which is why we should take him to hospital."

"And say what," snaps Chevy, "that you and this doctor you've never met cut him open on your kitchen table and performed an operation?"

"It was an emergency," she argues. "I have a duty of care if it's an emergency."

"Did you check the doctor's credentials?" he asks, smirking.

She glances helplessly at the doctor, who looks away. "Didn't you check them?"

"I don't need to," says Chevy. "I already know he's been struck off."

"What?" she screeches.

Chevy points to Logan. "And he's security at an underground fight that should not have taken place. And he ended up on your kitchen table. It looks to me like you're running in the wrong circles."

"Fuck you," she hisses.

"So, spare room?" he asks again.

She ties off the last stitch and goes over to the sink to wash her hands. "We'll find it," I say.

"Take another drink, Logan," says Chevy, holding the bottle of whiskey to his lips. He takes a few gulps, and we take a side each and ease him up off the table.

We help him up the stairs, and I let Chevy open each door until he finds the spare room. Once Logan is lying in the bed, we head out and leave the doctor to set up the drip again. "You'll need to stay here," says Chevy.

"Okay," I reply, nodding. At least I'll have a reason to be here with Xanthe.

"I'm gonna go back and update the boss," he adds. "Let me know if anything changes."

I follow him to the door, and once he's left, I go back into the kitchen, where Xanthe is scrubbing the table as the aroma of bleach fills the air. "I've got to stay here," I tell her. "Until Logan is well enough to leave."

"Great," she mutters.

"None of this is my fault," I tell her.

"I never said it was."

"But you're pissed with me."

"I'm pissed with all of you," she snaps. "Fuck." She slams her hands against the table.

I go to her and pull her against me. "We'll think of something."

"How? You can't even get yourself out of the shit with him."

"I'm only here cos my Pres wanted to punish me. Once I get back and tell him all this, he'll get me out."

"That doesn't mean he'll get me out," she mutters. "I really think we should go to the police."

I smile sadly, cupping her face until our eyes meet. "Xanth, it's not as easy as that. The police can't protect you from him."

"But you can?"

"I'm gonna try."

"What do you do for him, Reese? Why are you covered in blood?"

"It's Logan's blood," I lie. "We tried to help him, but there was too much claret, and we couldn't stop it."

We hear footsteps and break apart right as the doctor comes in. Placing some meds on the table, he states, "Painkillers, every four hours. If anything changes or he deteriorates, call me." I give a nod, and he leaves. I follow him, making sure to bolt the door.

When I return, Xanthe is looking at the label on the meds. "These are foreign," she says. "I don't even know what they are."

"You heard him—they're painkillers."

"I don't know that for sure, Reese. I'd be risking my licence if I give out unprescribed medication. Why was that man struck off?"

"I'll give them to Logan," I reassure her. "Don't worry."

"You won't answer my questions," she cries, her words laced with frustration.

I sigh heavily. "It won't help even if I do."

She shakes her head, her eyes full of sadness. "I need to shower," she mutters, heading for the stairs.

I nod, following. "I'll sit with Logan."

∼

I sleep in the chair in Logan's room. Xanthe doesn't come to find me, so I assume it's what she wants. When the sun rises, I give Logan his meds then go downstairs, where I find her at the kitchen table. She looks exhausted, and I offer a sympathetic smile which she doesn't return. I don't blame her. She associates me with Donnie.

"I need to go see my Pres," I tell her. "I've given Logan his medication. The doctor is calling in around nine. I should be back for then."

"Right," she mutters.

I sigh. "I'm going to find a solution, I promise."

∼

Axel sent a message last night to say church would be at eight. He's getting strict on shit like that, and if anyone shows late, he adds extra onto subs.

I take my seat and wait for everyone else to join. When we're all settled, Axel bangs the gavel. "Thought we should all check in," he begins. "Pit, you start."

Pit leans forward, resting his elbows on the table. "Not much going on, Pres. We're shifting the containers quickly, clearing the backlog."

"That's what I like to hear. I knew putting you in that role was a good idea." He turns to Cash. "Books looking good?"

Cash nods. "Yep. Checked in with the VP earlier this month, and he's happy," he says, looking at Grizz for confirmation, who nods.

"Dare I say it, but this is the quietest shit's been in a long time," says Axel, grinning. "I could get used to it." He turns to me. "But I know you're about to fuck it all up."

I sigh heavily. "Donnie is involved in some shit," I say. "I don't know what exactly, but it's bringing trouble to his club. In the early hours this morning, one of his men took a beating. He was stabbed."

"Fuck. Is he okay?" asks Nyx.

"I think he'll be okay. Donnie knew some doctor, although I'm not sure how legit he actually was. But I'm worried about Xanthe."

Axel groans. "Fucking women, every time," he mutters, and we all turn to him. "That's what brings us trouble," he explains. "Me and Lex, Grizz and Luna, Fletch and Gemma."

"Two of those women were cops," Grizz points out. "And Luna didn't bring anywhere near as much drama as Lexi."

"Hit me with it," says Axel, ignoring Grizz.

"Donnie has become obsessed with Xanthe," I say. "She's terrified. And now, he's sending injured men her way to patch up. Chevy made a veiled threat last night, said something about her being in too deep with criminals to refuse to help."

"I'd tell you ignore it," says Axel, "but I can already feel Coop glaring at me." A few of the men snigger, knowing Cooper always seems to advocate for women, maybe because his daughter is Lexi and he raised her alone. "What do you want us to do?"

I shrug. "I don't know, Pres. I can't leave her in the trenches."

"Because you want her?" asks Grizz.

I smirk. "Maybe. We have history, but if I go there right now, he'll come for me."

Nyx smirks. "Rumour has it, you already went there."

I glare at Fletch, who laughs. "And he almost caught me,"

I admit. "I don't want to give him an excuse to make this a competition."

"Maybe he'll get bored?" suggests Duke.

"Yeah, that's what I'm hoping," I reply. "He ordered we take Logan to her place to get patched up. She could lose her nursing licence if they carry on using her like that. I'm gonna try to get through to Donnie, but if shit goes south, I need to know you have my back," I say, fixing Axel with a stare.

"Of course, brother, you don't even have to ask. You know I only agreed to Donnie's proposal to teach you a lesson," he says. "I can pull you, and we'll deal with the fallout."

I shake my head. "Nah, I won't know what's going on if you do that."

"Alright." He nods. "Stay safe. And if you think she's in danger at any point, bring her to the clubhouse. He'd never come looking for her here, unless he knows you two have a past?"

I shake my head. "He doesn't know."

My mobile rings, and I see Donnie's name. "Speak of the devil." I stand and head out of church, answering the call.

"Pick me up from the club. I need to see Logan and find out who the fuck brought trouble." He disconnects, and I immediately call Xanthe, who answers straight away.

"Donnie wants me to bring him over to yours so he can quiz Logan."

"I thought he might make an appearance," she mutters.

"It's your chance to reiterate the message you sent him."

"He didn't even reply. I don't know if he saw it."

"He would have. We'll be there in about twenty minutes."

∼

THE FIRST THING I NOTICE WHEN WE ARRIVE BACK AT XANTHE'S is the huge bouquet of white roses on the kitchen worktop.

Donnie doesn't bother addressing her. Instead, he heads upstairs to where Logan is resting.

I follow and linger in the doorway as Donnie takes a seat by the bed. "Who was it?" I roll my eyes. He doesn't even bother to ask how Logan is. Axel can be a hard-faced fucker, but he always takes care of us over anything.

"Just kids," says Logan.

"Bullshit," spits Donnie, pushing to his feet. "You're telling me kids took you down, Logan? You!"

"Boss, they took me by surprise. There were at least ten of them, all masked-up."

"So, how do you know they were kids?" he demands.

Logan sighs. "I guess I don't for sure, but they seemed like kids. They were scrappy."

"Who do you think it was?" I ask, and Donnie turns to me, arching a brow. "Well, you seem sure it ain't kids, so do you have an idea?"

"If I did, I'm not likely to discuss it with you," he spits then heads downstairs.

Xanthe

I BRACE MYSELF THE SECOND I HEAR HIS FOOTSTEPS COMING down the stairs. Donnie stalks into the kitchen with purpose, kicking the door closed behind him so Fury can't follow, and then he pulls me into his arms, holding me tightly. I stiffen, keeping my arms at my sides.

"I missed you," he whispers, pressing his lips to the side of my head.

"Donnie," I whisper, trying to pull away.

"It's been a rough few hours," he adds, still not releasing me.

I manage to get my hands between us, and I push hard,

forcing him to release me. "I texted you," I state, moving around the worktop to keep space between us.

He looks mildly irritated and places his hands on the counter, fixing me with a stern stare. "We talked about this already."

"Yes, but you're not listening to me, Donnie. You brought a man to my house. He's sleeping in my fucking spare room."

"Don't get hysterical," he mutters, rolling his eyes.

"Look, you need to leave, and you need to take that man with you."

"That's not possible," he says, pulling out his mobile and staring down at it.

"It's not a fucking request, Donnie. Get him out, and don't bother me again or I will call the police."

He throws his mobile on the worktop and rounds it so quick, I almost fall onto my backside trying to back away from him. His hand dashes out, grabbing my throat, and as if I weigh nothing, he lifts me and slams me onto the table. I wince as pain radiates through me, shock causing me to freeze up. I stare wide-eyed as he sneers down at me.

"Hey, Donnie, stop, stop." I realise Fury is in the room trying to prise Donnie's hand from my neck. He eventually releases me, and I cough violently, rolling onto my side. "Jesus, what the fuck are you doing?"

"You're right," says Donnie, calmly. He holds out his hand for me to take, but I stare at it with contempt until he retracts it. "I'm sorry. I overreacted."

"I want him to leave," I say firmly, glaring at Fury. "Now."

Donnie's anger returns. He switches so quick, I feel sick with panic. Narrowing his eyes, he snaps, "You want Logan gone?"

"Yes," I say clearly.

He turns on his heel and marches towards the stairs. Fury winces. "Oh fuck," he whispers, rushing after Donnie.

I go to the bottom of the stairs, confused as I hear Fury

trying desperately to talk Donnie down. "Boss, not like this," he hisses. "Come on, relax. She's just upset."

I take the stairs two at a time, furious he's answering for me. I'm not some unhinged, upset woman who'll get over this. I want him out of my life and Logan out of my house. I stop in the doorway, my mouth falling open at the sight of Donnie kneeling over Logan, who is gurgling with blood pouring from his mouth. It takes a second for my brain to engage, but when it does, I scream. Donnie laughs—actually laughs—before pushing off the bed and tucking his knife away.

"What did you do?" I cry, grabbing a clean sheet from the end of the bed and pressing it over the gaping wound on Logan's neck. "Oh my god." Usually, I'm calm in emergencies and know exactly what to do. But as Logan stares into my eyes, the life draining from him, I'm suddenly lost. I have no idea how to stop this man dying. He takes one last gasp and then falls silent. "No," I cry desperately. "No, no, no."

"Xanthe, it's too late," Fury whispers gently, and then his hands grip my wrists and remove them from Logan's neck. "He's gone."

"No," I repeat, staring at Logan's open eyes. "Oh god."

"Shall we talk downstairs?" asks Donnie, smiling before leaving the room.

I begin to hyperventilate. I can't seem to fill my lungs with air, and as they tighten, I gasp harder. "Relax," says Fury, bending slightly at the knee to look me in the eye. "It's okay," he adds. "Breathe slow, in through the nose and out through the mouth."

I scowl, shoving him from me and crouching down to rest my forehead on my knees. I squeeze my eyes closed and focus on my breathing. *How fucking dare he tell me to relax?* Relax! I've just gotten the man killed. I lift my head and look directly at Logan's hand hanging limply off the edge of the bed. "Oh god," I whisper again. "What have I done?"

"Look, we have to go downstairs or things will just get worse," says Fury.

"Worse?" I hiss, pushing to my feet. "He just fucking killed a man in my spare room. How can it get any worse?" I storm from the room and head downstairs to find Donnie waiting patiently in the kitchen.

"Have you had time to process?" he asks casually.

I don't think, acting clearly on anger as I pull my hand back and slap him hard. He doesn't react. Instead, he smiles again while rubbing his cheek. "What do you want?" I ask, folding my arms over my chest and avoiding his evil eyes.

"Candice Bowman . . . she's your boss, right?" He moves closer to me, taking my chin between his thumb and finger and tilting my head so we're eye-to-eye. "I can be patient, Xanthe, until you're ready. But for now, I'll settle with your help."

"Help?" I repeat, still reeling from how he knows my boss's name.

"Friday and Saturday nights are fight nights at the club. You'll patch the fighters up."

"But I can't do that," I begin, frowning.

"I've arranged for your shifts to work around when I require you."

I gasp. "What?"

"Like I've said, I know people."

"What people? Why the hell are you messing with my job?" I pull my chin free and glance back at Fury lingering in the doorway. He looks angry. I can tell by the subtle way his jaw is clenched and how the vein in his forehead is protruding a little. "Do something," I demand angrily.

"He works for me, Xanthe. No one is going to rescue you," sneers Donnie. I pull my glare away from Fury and focus back on the monster before me. "You have no choice but to agree." He looks happy, and I wonder how I never noticed the way his eyes twinkle with an evil glint. Maybe because his true happiness is causing others misery.

"What did I ever do to you?" I whisper sadly.

His hand cups the back of my head, and he slams his mouth against mine. I push against his chest, but he only holds me firmer until I stop struggling. When he finally pulls away, I wipe my mouth on the back of my hand. "Disgusting," I hiss.

He chuckles. "I'll be in touch."

He heads for the door, and my heart slams hard in my chest. I rush after him, grabbing his arm until he's forced to slow. "Wait," I cry. "What about the . . . the body upstairs?"

His grin only widens. "Fury will help you." And then he shrugs free and leaves. I stare after him, waiting until the door slams closed before I slowly turn to Fury.

"What the fuck just happened?"

CHAPTER 8

Fury

"We need to find you somewhere to stay," I mutter. "Let me call Axel."

"Are you being serious?"

I spin on her, allowing my anger to take over. The fact she's been exposed to all this is sending me over the edge. I should have stepped in sooner to avoid her getting so involved. "He just killed a man in front of you," I yell. "He's not going to let you walk away."

I head into the kitchen, and she rushes after me. "What do you mean?"

"We need bleach," I say, ignoring her panic-stricken face. "Clean every surface in here. Get rid of any trace of Logan."

"What about his body?" she asks, tears filling her eyes. "We should call the police."

"Don't you get it?" I snap. "You're in too deep, Xanthe. Fuck!" I run my fingers through my hair and turn my back on her. "I told you to stay the fuck away from him," I mutter.

"So, this is my fault?" she cries.

I turn back to her as she swipes angrily at the tears that have escaped and stained her cheeks. "No, it's just . . ." I groan. "If you'd have listened, we wouldn't be here now. But we are, so find some bleach and I'll call Axel."

I step into the back garden and close the door before dialling my President off my burner phone. He answers on the second ring. "How's things?"

"Bad. Very bad," I reply. "Can you get the clean-up here urgently?"

"It's the middle of the day," he says. "What's happened? Fuck, you haven't ended Donnie, have you?"

I frown. "No, but it might be a possibility very soon."

"We've done some digging, and we're hearing some bad shit."

"He ended Logan," I mutter, "in front of Xanthe."

"Fuck."

"He's lost his mind. We both know it means she can't walk away."

"He'll end her," says Axel.

"Exactly. He wants her working for him on the weekends, patching up some of the fighters."

"You have to get her out of there."

"I plan to." I stare through the kitchen window just as the front door opens and Chevy walks in. "I gotta go. His man's just walked in. Hold on with the clean-up."

"I'll have a room set up for her."

I disconnect and head inside. Chevy points to a box, and I already know it contains the shit I use to clean up. "Thought you'd need this."

"I can't get rid of a body in the fucking day," I snap. "I'll sort it later."

"Boss insisted I stick around."

I frown. "Why?"

"To make sure the clean-up goes well."

"What are you talking about?" I snap. "He's never been bothered before."

"She was never involved before," he replies, and I glance over to where Xanthe is scrubbing the worktop while staring into space.

"She's not getting involved now," I hiss, stepping closer.

"You think there's a choice?" he asks with a smirk. "I've lined some bags to stop him . . . leaking out all over the place. I'll grab them from the car. Get him in those and we'll take them to the car as soon as it's dark."

"This is fucked-up," I mutter, shaking my head.

"Look, he needs her to do this so she can't go screaming to the police," he hisses.

"She's in shock. She ain't gonna call anyone," I snap. "Look at her."

"I'm following orders," he says, holding up his hands. "Unless you wanna end up like Logan, I suggest you do the same."

"He liked Logan," I say, frowning deeper. "He was pissed when he got hurt and made sure we got him straight here for help."

Chevy scoffs. "Don't get it twisted, Fury. He don't care about anyone . . ." He pauses to look at Xanthe. "Except her," he says thoughtfully, "and if she doesn't start catching feelings soon, it'll be her you're cutting up next."

I wait for him to go out to the car before grabbing Xanthe by her upper arms. She startles like she wasn't aware I was in the room. "Xanth, listen," I say firmly, "this is really important."

She blinks a few times and nods. "You have to help me with Logan," I say, waiting a beat to see if she understands what I'm saying. "Dispose of him," I add.

She tries to back away, shaking her head vigorously. "Xanth, there's no choice. Donnie's sent his hitman to watch us."

"I can't," she says desperately. "I can't do that." Her eyes are wide with panic, and she's still shaking her head.

"I can't get us out of this, Xanthe," I say desperately. "Chevy carries a gun, I don't. My fists won't protect us from him when he's come prepared."

"Oh my god," she whispers. "I don't think I can, Reese. Honestly, I can't stop thinking about him."

"We don't have time to talk about it," I snap. "He'll be back any second."

"You don't understand," she cries, now beginning to shake uncontrollably. "I can't."

"If you don't, he's going to put a bullet in you next."

She covers her face with her hands and sobs. Hard, heavy sobs rack her body, and my heart twists painfully. "I swear, after today, you'll never see him again. You just have to get through this."

The front door swings open, and I instantly back away. "Are we ready?" asks Chevy.

I grab the box. "Yep," I say, heading upstairs.

"And you," I hear him say to Xanthe.

Upstairs, I dump the box on the floor and open it. I get out the plastic sheet and lay it beside the bed. Xanthe walks in looking pale and exhausted. Her hands are still shaking, and her eyes are red and puffy from her tears.

I take hold of Logan and roll him from the bed. He lands with a deafening thud, and Xanthe immediately slams her hands over her mouth and turns away slightly. "You're a nurse," says Chevy from the doorway. "You've seen bodies before."

"Fuck you," she mutters.

He grins and steps farther into the room before taking a seat in the rocking chair in the corner. "I'm going to enjoy this."

I catch Xanthe's eye and give my head a slight shake, warning her to ignore him. He's trying to rile her, and I'm sure he'd love nothing more than to end her so his boss's attention is back to where it should be.

I hand Xanthe a set of goggles. I never use them, but I sense she might want to cover up as much as possible. I shrug from my kutte and lay it at the end of the bed before dropping to my knees beside the body and grabbing a saw. "What are you doing?" she asks, backing away until she hits the wall.

"Don't look at it like a body," I mutter, not meeting her eyes. I place the saw down and use a pair of scissors to cut away Logan's shirt. "Pretend it's a lump of meat."

Xanthe gags, covering her mouth with her hands. "This can't be happening."

"Some people strip down to their underwear," Chevy suggests with a grin. "Less mess."

"Are you suggesting I do that?" she snaps.

He shrugs. "If you want to, that's cool."

"She's not fucking stripping off," I snap.

I grab the saw and begin cutting at Logan's elbow. Chevy's mobile rings and he stands. "I gotta take this," he says as he leaves the room.

Xanthe crouches down and hisses, "Why are you looking so comfortable doing this?"

"Let's just get the job done so I can get you out of here," I whisper.

"You've done this before," she accuses.

"That's what you want to discuss right now?" I snap. "My body count?"

She gasps. "There's a body count?"

"Look, Xanth, I know you have questions—of course, you do—but now isn't the time. So, let's get this bagged up so we can leave."

"And then what?" she asks.

"And then I'll answer all your questions."

"Promise?"

"I swear it."

She gives a stiff nod and grabs the nearest bag, holding it open so I can drop in the lower arm.

Xanthe

I'VE TOUCHED DEAD BODIES BEFORE, AS IT'S PART OF MY JOB. AND there, in the hospital, I can shut it off. Maybe it's something I learned to do without even realising it. It's not like anyone pulled me to one side when I was training and offered me words of wisdom—it just came as part and parcel. But as I watch Fury cut off each part from Logan's body, I want to scream. There's a rage burning deep inside me that is desperately trying to get out. How did I even get here?

Chevy comes back in. "Did you remove his fingertips?" he asks, holding the phone to his chest.

Fury gives a frustrated sigh. "No. Aren't we doing the usual?"

"He said remove them," he replies, shrugging. He leaves again, and Fury reaches into the tool bag to retrieve a pair of pliers.

"What's the usual?" I ask. He glances up then pulls the lower limb from the bag and proceeds to snip off Logan's fingertips, letting them fall carelessly onto the plastic sheet. "Reese?" I push.

"Burning the body," he mutters.

"And if they're not burning him, how will they get rid of him?"

He shrugs. "I don't know, Xanthe, it's not my job to ask questions."

"But it's your job to cut people up into bits?" My voice wavers with emotion. How did he end up here? My Reese. Sweet, kind, Reese. The boy who kissed my knees when I fell and comforted me when my parents got to be too much.

"I don't know what you want me to say, Xanthe. This isn't exactly my job. I don't do this part. But, yeah, I end lives. That's part of my job."

"What happened to you?" I whisper, allowing more tears to trail down my cheeks.

"To make me so cold?" he asks with a sneer. "Maybe I was always like this."

I shake my head. "No, you weren't."

He scoffs, "Because you knew me so well?"

"Yes."

He laughs, but it's cold and empty as he hacks off the upper arm. "You knew what I wanted you to know."

"That's not true."

He drops the saw and pushes to his feet, getting in my face. "I wanted your parents to like me, Xanth. I wanted to stay in one fucking place for once because I was so damn tired of being moved from one home to the next, no one ever taking the time to bother getting to know me because all they cared about was the money they made from fostering a kid like me. So, I put on a front where I pretended to be kind and thoughtful. I was being the kid everyone needed me to be so I could be loved. Turns out, that didn't fucking work, so I learned the hard way that no matter what you do or say, you can't escape your past. You can't pretend you weren't abandoned over and over until it eats you away inside." He's so angry, his face is red, and spittle flies from his mouth. "So, no, Xanthe, you didn't fucking know me at all." He drops back to his knees and continues to saw through bone.

I turn and run from the room. I can't take another second acting like everything he's doing in there is normal. Even if it is in his world.

Chevy looks up in surprise as I shove past him and go into my bedroom, locking the door. I lean against it, sliding down until my backside hits the floor. I pull my knees to my chest and rest my forehead against them.

He's lying. What we had was special. He wasn't pretending when he was with me. I know it.

I lie on my side, closing my eyes. I need all this to just go away now.

∼

I wake with a start, instantly groaning as I uncurl myself, realising I'm still on the floor. I push to sit up, looking around in bewilderment. It's dark outside, which means I must have been asleep for the last few hours.

A knock on the door startles me, and I realise that's what woke me. "Xanthe, come out. We have to leave."

I push to my feet and unlock the door. Fury is pacing with worry etched on his face. He exhales in relief when he lays eyes on me then places his hands on my face. I instantly pull back, causing his hands to fall to his sides. His words hurt me, and he can't pretend he didn't say them.

He sighs again, this time placing his hands on his hips. I note he's changed his clothes. "You need to pack a bag."

"Where are we going?"

"To the clubhouse."

"I can't hide forever. What if he comes there to find me?"

"He won't. He doesn't know we know one another, and I left with Chevy earlier, so as far as they know, you're here in your bedroom."

"Where's Logan?" I ask, shuddering as images assault my brain.

He goes to the spare room and pushes the door open. I step closer, looking inside. It's clean, like he was never there. "All gone."

"From the house maybe, but not from here," I mutter, tapping my head.

"Yeah, that takes a while to fade."

"What time is it?" I ask.

He checks his watch. "Six."

"I need to see my mum." He begins to shake his head. "I have to. I always go for dinner on Wednesday, and she's expecting me. I can't cancel half an hour before I'm meant to be there."

"I don't want to leave your side," he admits, staring at the ground. It's another glimpse of his vulnerability. A reminder that I do know him, despite what he'd said.

"Then come with me."

"She won't want to see me," he mutters.

"She might surprise you," I reply, going back into my room and rummaging through my drawers until I find a pair of jeans and a jumper. I change quickly before taking a bag from under my bed and packing for a few nights.

Once I have what I think I'll need, we head out. Fury makes sure the coast is clear as we get into the car he drives for Donnie, one I've been in many times. I shudder, realising how utterly stupid I've been.

I tap my mum's address into Fury's phone satnav and then pull out my mobile and call my mum, ignoring Fury's curious glance as he drives. "Hi, Mum," I say the minute she answers. "Is there room for one more?"

"You know I always cook for an army," she jokes. "Are you bringing Jorja?"

"No, it's a surprise," I say, forcing myself to sound like I'm happy.

"Oh, does this mean it's a man? Is it the one you told me about?" She sounds excited, and now, I feel like a shit because I don't know if she's going to be happy to see Fury. Not after what he's told me.

"No, it's not him. You know this guy. We'll be there in twenty minutes."

Once I disconnect, I tuck my phone away and rest my head against the window. I have a thumping headache, and

I'm so tired despite having slept uncomfortably on the floor for a few hours.

"I know it all seems like a lot right now," says Fury gently, "but I swear it'll get better."

"When?"

"I don't know," he mutters.

"Then don't make stupid promises," I snap, and we fall into silence for the rest of the journey.

He stops two streets away from Mum's place, telling me he's not sure if Donnie's vehicles are tracked. I twist in my seat and take a deep breath. "I have to act normal in front of my mum," I say. "She knows me well, and she'll sense I'm upset about something, so I'm going to say I broke up with Donnie and pretend I'm devastated."

"You told her about him?" he asks, and I see in his eyes it bothers him.

"Yes."

"And now you're going to act heartbroken," he mutters bitterly.

"Yes, and then I'm going to say you turned up at the hospital today."

He scoffs. "And you thought you'd invite me to dinner?"

"Yes. She knows how upset I was when you left. She'd fully expect me to welcome you home, where I always knew you belonged." He rolls his eyes and gets out the car. I sigh and then follow. "You have to lose the attitude before we go in there," I snap.

"She knows how it went down in the end," I snap. "Me and her, we both sat at that table whilst your dad told me I was gonna leave. I promised to stay away."

"That was years ago. Besides, you showed up at the hospital. You weren't to know I'd be there. She'll assume I've been my usual persistent self and forced you into this."

"You have," he mutters.

I march off towards her house, leaving him to trail behind me.

Mum greets me in the usual way, wrapping me tightly in her arms. Only this time, I recognise the second she spots Fury because she stiffens slightly, and I think I hear a slight gasp. She releases me, her eyes firmly fixed past me and on him. "Surprise," I say with forced enthusiasm. "Look who I ran into."

"Reese," she almost whispers.

"Hey, Dianna. How are you?" His voice is off. It sounds empty of emotion, and for the first time, I think about how hard this might be for him. But it's too late now, so I smile wide.

"He was at the hospital."

"Are you hurt?" she asks, moving past me to him, where she holds him at arm's length and scans him with her eyes. I feel a warmness spread through my heart watching how she checks him over, like he never left her sight. He towers over her small frame, but it doesn't seem to bother her as she reaches up to cup his cheek. "You've grown into a big, strong lad," she comments. "I knew you would. Now, come inside. Let's eat and you can tell me everything."

CHAPTER 9

Fury

I stare in wonderment as Dianna goes back inside followed by Xanthe. I should be angry. The seventeen-year-old boy inside me should be even more angry. But I find myself following them like the desperate, unloved kid I've always been because I need her approval. I need her to smile at me with the warmth I remember before she turfed me out.

I close the door and turn to the walls adorned with hundreds of pictures of every kid they've ever fostered. They had the same 'wall of fame', as Xanthe called it, at the last place. And the same scent—the smell of food mixed with a sweet hint of honeysuckle. Whenever I smell the flower, I'm reminded of this family. It makes me feel safe, like a comfort blanket.

I step into the kitchen, where Xanthe is flicking through a pile of mail and Dianna is stirring what looks like gravy. "I need someone strong to carve the beef," she tells me, nodding to where the meat is resting on the worktop.

I head over and pick up the carving knife. I feel Xanthe's wide eyes on me, just like when she watched me earlier.

"So," says Dianna, smiling, "what do you do for work?"

Xanthe brings her eyes to mine, and I look away, returning Dianna's smile. "I'm a boxer. I work some shifts at a gym and do occasional bar work."

"You're busy then," she remarks. "You always had to be on the go. What about marriage or kids?"

I shake my head and stick the long-pronged fork into the joint. "Nah, I haven't met the one yet."

She looks away before clearing her throat. "I always wondered about you," she says. "I called the family you went to after a few weeks had passed. The social worker said to wait at least a month to let you settle." She smiles sadly. "When they said you'd run away, I was . . . well, it broke my heart. I called the police several times, but they didn't seem bothered, said you were a troubled kid and you'd only keep doing it if they returned you. But they promised to contact me if you showed up."

Xanthe frowns, staring at her mum in shock. "I didn't know any of that."

Dianna looks guilty. "You didn't know half of it," she mutters. "So, Reese, where did you end up?"

"From Manchester, I went to Liverpool, met some friends, and then went to Nottingham. I was there for a long time, and then I met a guy who took me in at the motorcycle club. I moved here a few months ago."

"What a coincidence," she says, smiling again. "All this time you've been here, and we haven't seen you until now."

"I've been busy."

"Well, you weren't to know we were here," she pauses before adding, "I'm not sure you'd have bothered to look us up anyway."

"It was a long time ago," I mutter. "I'm over it."

She eyes me for a few seconds before nodding at the meat. "Carve it thinly. I hate chewing it."

"Mum, Reese rides a motorbike," says Xanthe brightly.

Dianna chuckles. "You had an eye for danger too. A thrill seeker, I used to tell your social worker."

"I like the freedom that comes with it," I explain.

"I can picture it," she says wistfully. "You on a bike, enjoying the road and all that freedom. You were like a caged animal when you first arrived. Wouldn't sit still." She gives a sad laugh. "You know, every time a child leaves, you take something on board. A piece of knowledge, a thought that relates to that child, and you . . ." She places her hands on the kitchen worktop and fixes me with a firm stare. "Well, when you left, I had nothing. Maybe it was because I was so sad, but you're the only child I've thought about a lot, that I've spent time wondering about." Dianna sets three plates on the worktop and begins to dish dinner up. "Go take a seat at the table," she instructs.

I follow Xanthe through to the dining room leading off from the kitchen, Dianna's words ringing in my ears. Knowing she thought about me warms me a little. I'd just assumed she was glad to see the back of me.

"This is awkward," I whisper, sitting at the table.

"Not as awkward as some of the stuff I've witnessed today," she retorts, sitting beside me.

"I had to do what I had to do," I reply. "Otherwise, we wouldn't have walked out of there alive."

She twists in her seat to look at me. "Okay, so how many times have you done that?"

"You choose the worst times to discuss this sorta thing," I mutter, shaking my head in annoyance. The truth is, I don't want to discuss it at all. She's not happy with it, and once she knows the truth, she'll want to be far away from me, and I'm not ready for that.

Dianna comes in carrying two plates stacked with roast

beef, potatoes, and vegetables. "Tuck in," she says with a smile as she places one down before each of us. "Gravy is coming," she adds, going into the kitchen again. She returns seconds later with her own dinner and a gravy jug. I take it and pour some over my dinner. It's been way too long since I had a homecooked food like this, and I'm desperate to get stuck in.

"How's work?" Dianna asks Xanthe.

"Same old," she replies. "Busy. I'm taking a few days off actually."

"You are?"

Xanthe nods. "I broke up with Donnie, so I thought I'd spend some time catching up with Reese."

Dianna's eyes flit between us before she forces a smile. "Well, makes sense. You were practically brother and sister."

I shudder, dropping my fork back on my plate and pushing it away slightly. Xanthe arches a brow and smirks. "Really, Mum?"

"Don't do this now, Xanth," I warn.

She ignores me, glaring at her mum, who stares back with a look of guilt on her face. "I know what happened," Xanthe continues. "I know you sent him away."

Dianna shakes her head. "It wasn't just down to me."

"Okay, so when Dad read the riot act, you did everything you could to stop him, right?"

"It was a hard decision," snaps Dianna. "We didn't know what to do, and we agonised over it for hours. But in the end, we had to put you first."

"Putting me first would've meant keeping Reese with us."

"We didn't know the rules on it all," says Dianna desperately. "We didn't know if it would all come out and affect our fostering chances."

"Oh god, so you sent him away because you didn't want to mess up your clean record?"

"That's not true," Dianna yells angrily. "I loved that boy like my own."

I hang my head and take a few deep breaths. I've never felt parental love like I did when I lived with Dianna, and her words are a painful reminder of everything I lost.

"I loved him," Xanthe screams, and my head shoots up in surprise. "And you sent him away and broke my heart." She bursts into tears, and I grab her hand, gently squeezing it.

Dianna fights to hold her tears in. "I hated myself," she whispers. "And if I could change it, I would."

"It's in the past," I state. "I didn't mean to come back and cause problems." I push to stand, releasing Xanthe's hand. "Again."

"Where are you going?" Xanthe sniffles.

"Finish your dinner. I'm gonna wait outside."

"Don't be ridiculous."

"It was good to see you again, Dianna. Sorry for the trouble."

I head for the door. "Wait," Dianna demands, and I pause, turning back. "Let me explain, please."

I sigh heavily. It's been a rough day and I'm exhausted, but the plea in her eyes has me nodding in agreement. She points to my seat, so I lower back into it. "I tried to keep you," she admits. "I knew Xanth would be heartbroken, and I argued with Mack over the decision. I hate to put the blame on him when he can't defend himself, but he was adamant it wouldn't work. I wanted to wait and see, but he was worried you'd both fall out and things would get ugly." She sighs heavily. "I told him that young love was messy, and if you didn't break her heart, someone else would. But she was his baby girl, and he wanted to protect her. He felt you'd disrespected us by sneaking around."

"It wasn't his fault," says Xanthe.

"It's fine," I cut in.

"No, it's not," she snaps. "Mum, I wouldn't take no for an

answer. I liked him and I wanted to be with him. He said no because he liked living with us. He didn't want to risk it."

Dianna smiles. "I knew it would be down to you and your demanding ways."

"If I'd have known what would happen, I would've waited."

"And if I'd have known how much you liked one another, I'd have fought harder." She brings her eyes to me. "I'm so sorry if you felt abandoned." Her voice breaks, and a sob escapes her. She slaps her hand over her mouth. "It haunted me for years after. When I knew you'd run off, it broke my heart, and Mack's. He was racked with guilt."

I reach a hand over the table and take hers. Knowing the truth feels good, like a weight is lifted. "I'm sorry too. I should've come to you and talked about it."

"The past is the past," she states, using her free hand to wipe her tears away. "What's important is the future, and I hope you'll stick around so we can get to know you again."

I give a nod, and she smiles wide. "And maybe . . . with you both being single . . ."

"Mum," Xanthe screeches, "stop."

"I'm just saying that maybe some things are meant to be."

Xanthe

We finish dinner while Fury tells Mum all about boxing. I sit back and listen to how animated and passionate he is, wondering why we haven't talked about any of that. Apart from all the drama, I know nothing about his life now. I make a mental note to spend the next couple days putting that right.

We spend an hour with Mum before it's time to head off. Fury drives us to the clubhouse, and once we park up, I turn to him. "I'm terrified," I admit.

"Relax, they're all pussycats."

"Not just of the club," I mutter. "What if he finds out I'm here, that you've hidden me?"

"I can handle Donnie Nelson," he says with a grin. "But I want to do this right so you get to walk away with no blowback."

"And then what?"

He shrugs. "Then you walk away."

"From everything, including you?"

A man approaches the car, breaking our stare-off. Fury climbs out and shakes hands with him. "Fletch, this is Xanthe."

The man stoops down slightly to peer into the car before grinning. "I knew you'd be hot."

Fury clips him around the ear. "Show some fucking respect or I'll tell Gemma."

He rubs the spot, grinning as he stands fully again. "Pres got a room made up for you both."

I get out the car. "Separate, I hope," I say, arching a brow.

"Huh, I like her," says Fletch, heading for the building.

Inside, I'm introduced to other men before a woman heads my way holding out a hand, and we shake. "I'm Lexi."

"Xanthe," I reply.

"Once you're settled, come find me and I'll show you around."

Fury grabs my hand. "It can wait until tomorrow, Lex. We've had the longest day."

He leads me upstairs and along a hall. We reach a room, and he pushes the door open, indicating for me to go inside. "Your room," he says, following me in. "I'll be through there," he adds, pointing to a conjoining door which he also opens to show his bedroom. "I'll keep it closed to give you privacy."

I can't help feeling disappointed that we're not sharing, even though I'm the one making it clear I want him at a distance. I give a stiff nod and place my bag on the floor. "Thanks."

"I'll let you get settled." He heads for his door.

"Actually," I say, and he pauses, "we should talk."

"It's been a long day," he mutters, keeping his back to me. "When we finally talk, it'll be with clear heads."

"But I have questions and—"

He turns back to me, closing the gap between us in a flash and pressing his lips to mine. I freeze up, shocked as he gently slides his hand to cup my cheek. He pulls back slightly to look me in the eyes. "You're far too stubborn for your own good. Goodnight, Xanthe." And he leaves, closing the door that separates us.

I stare after him. *What was that? A goodnight kiss? A friendship kiss?* I narrow my eyes in annoyance before following him. I push the door with more force than I mean too, taking him by surprise. He's topless, folding his shirt. We stare at one another, and something passes between us, a charge of some kind that pulls me to him. I throw myself at him, and he catches me, lifting me. My arms tangle around his neck as I slam my mouth to his, swiping my tongue into his mouth and kissing him with everything I have.

I feel his mobile vibrate in his pocket right before it shrills noisily. He breaks the kiss, lowering my feet to the floor and stepping back. His eyes linger on mine for a few seconds before he releases a long breath and pulls out his mobile, accepting the call.

"Yep?" He waits, listening to whoever is on the other end before disconnecting. He grabs his shirt, pulling it on hastily. "I have to go."

I frown, following him around the room while he collects his keys and wallet. "Where?" He stuffs his feet back into his boots.

"That was Chevy. Donnie wants to see me."

My eyes widen with panic, and I make a grab for his arm.

He stills, his eyes landing on where my hand grips his wrist tightly. I release it and take a breath. "About what?"

"He didn't say."

"More clean-up jobs?"

"I'll see you later." He heads for the door, and I feel my heart tighten. I don't want him to go, and I don't trust Donnie.

"You're better than that, yah know," I say, and he pauses. "Being Donnie's bitch." It's a low blow, but if I have to cause an argument to keep him here, I will.

He sniggers, shaking his head with disappointment before pulling the door open and leaving.

Minutes pass and I'm still rooted to the spot, wondering what Donnie wants with Fury, when the door swings open and Lexi comes in with another woman. "Fury sent us up to keep you company," she announces.

I smile sadly. "I'm not much company, to be honest."

"When you feel shit, it's the best time for company," says the other woman heading into my room through the conjoining door.

"That's Luna," Lexi explains, following her.

I go into the room and close the middle door. The women are sitting on my bed, watching me expectantly. "You have that lost look," says Luna. "Are you and Fury . . ." She trails off.

"No," I rush to say, shaking my head a little too vigorously. The women exchange a smirk.

"But you want to be?" Luna guesses.

I feel myself blushing. "No. We're friends. At least, we were." I add a small, unamused laugh. "I don't even know him anymore."

"We don't know him that well," says Lexi. "He only came here a few months ago."

"Yeah, he's a closed book, hard to open," adds Luna, nodding.

"Maybe I shouldn't speak about him," I say hesitantly. I don't think he'd like me talking about his past, otherwise, he'd have told them already.

Lexi shrugs. "So, how did you meet him?"

"We met as teenagers," I say, trying not to give too much away. "And then we lost touch, and he turned up a few weeks back in the hospital."

"You work there?" asks Luna.

I nod. "I'm a nurse."

"Handy," says Lexi. "You should be wary hanging out in these places. They tend to take advantage."

I smirk. "Kind of too late for that."

She sits straighter. "Is Axel using you?"

I shake my head. "No, not him." She visibly relaxes. "A guy I met. Donnie."

"And Fury is trying to help you?" Luna guesses.

"Yeah, but this guy . . . he's bad news. I'm worried how deep Fury is already, and now he's helping me . . ." I trail off, and Lexi gently places her hand over mine.

"These bikers are tougher than you think," she says. "Fury can handle it, and anything he can't, the club will."

I groan. "Exactly my point. All these people are getting dragged into my mess." I bury my face in my hands. "How did I end up like this?"

"Let me guess. Sweet, charming guy turns out to be a complete headache?" asks Luna. I nod, and she grins. "It's standard bum magnet behaviour."

Lexi laughs. "That's not a thing."

"It really is," says Luna with confidence. "Some of us just attract the wrong sort, like wolves in sheep's clothing."

"I always did love a bad boy," I huff.

"So, what's this Donnie guy done that's so crazy?" asks Lexi.

I chew on my lower lip. Fury never said I couldn't tell anyone, but doing so might get him into trouble. After all, I have no idea who these women really are, or if the club shares this sort of stuff with their other halves. But right now, I need to talk about it, and Fury isn't willing to.

"I met him a few weeks ago. He was really nice, and I liked him instantly. But then Fury warned me off him, said he was a bad guy. I didn't really take much notice, but when I tried to take a step back, Donnie seemed really clingy. And now, because I want to break things off, he's forcing me to do stuff for him."

"Like?" Luna presses, concern on her face.

"He arranges fights," I say.

"Underground fights?" asks Lexi. "Illegal ones?"

I nod. "And he wants me to fix the fighters up after."

"You could lose your nursing licence," Lexi says.

"Exactly. There's something else." They both wait for me to continue. "He brought a fighter to my house. He was really hurt. Donnie killed him in my spare room." I slap my hand over my mouth as a sob escapes me. I thought I'd done all my crying, but being here in the safety of this club makes me want to offload. Lexi immediately pulls me into her arms.

"Shit. Does Fury know?"

"Yes," I say, taking a deep, shaky breath. "Fury cleans up the bodies." I sit back, and the women exchange a look that isn't shocked. "You know?"

Lexi shrugs. "Not really. Not details. But we're not stupid. We know the club isn't legit."

"And you're okay with it?" I ask, my throat tightening with more tears.

"We trust our men," declares Luna.

I scoff. "You sound like Stepford wives."

"I was a police officer," says Lexi, and I gasp. "I tried to take down the club."

"Newsflash, you failed," I state, and she laughs.

"I realised Axel wasn't a bad man," she says. "None of them are." I know she's right. Fury isn't bad either, but he's involved in things I want to walk away from. "It's the life they lead," she adds, "and it takes an understanding woman to love a man who wants to make a difference using unethical means."

"It's not the life for me," I say firmly. "I can't sleep next to a man who hours earlier had chopped up a dead body and helped dispose of it like it meant nothing."

"What if that body belonged to a bad person?" asks Luna. "Like Donnie?"

"He's got a screw loose, for sure," I say, "but murder is a little extreme." I shake my head in disbelief. I thought speaking to these women would ease my worries, but they're essentially telling me to accept it. I give an unamused laugh. "What am I saying?" I ask. "It's not like Fury even wants me. I just wanted a better life for him, yah know?"

"That's your first mistake," says Lexi, pushing to her feet. "Thinking this life isn't perfect for him. Ask him if he's happy, Xanthe. Just because it's not the life we know doesn't make it wrong." She heads for the door. "Get some rest."

CHAPTER 10

Fury

It's been a long-arse night, and right now, all I want is to fall into bed and sleep. But when I open my door, I find Xanthe sleeping in my bed. She's curled up in a ball on her side, her back to me, her breathing steady. I sigh heavily. I'd spent years wanting this exact thing. Having her in my bed was a fantasy I never thought would happen again, yet here she is, and it would be easy to slip in beside her and wrap her in my arms. But making her mine would just trap her. I saw it written all over her face earlier—she's disappointed in me, in what I've become. But this club is the only family I've known, and there's no way I can turn my back.

I go into my bathroom, pushing the door to before flicking the light on. I stare at my reflection in the mirror above the sink, taking in my white T-shirt which is now stained red. It doesn't faze me. I like it. But it's another reminder of how different Xanthe and I are.

I shrug from my kutte and place it on the hook behind the

door. Next, I pull off my T-shirt and dump it on the floor. Slipping from my jeans, I turn the shower on and wait for the steam to billow out before stepping under the spray. I close my eyes as the water washes away my latest sins.

It's her hands that startle me as they wrap around my waist. They're cold against the heat of my body. "I was worried about you," she whispers against my back.

I wait a second to reply, enjoying the way she feels against me. "You don't need to worry about me," I tell her, scared to turn around, knowing my body will betray me. "I can look after myself."

She releases me, but I keep my back to her. She takes the soap from the dish, then slips around me so she's in front, her innocent eyes staring up at me unblinking as the water soaks her silk short pyjamas. Her nipples pebble tightly, begging me to taste them.

She rubs her hands over the soap, dropping it back in the dish, then she tentatively places each hand against my solid chest. I inhale sharply, watching as she slowly rubs them over my wet skin in small circular motions. "You were gone a long time." She looks down between us, watching the blood wash away. My erection stands proudly, and she glances back up, biting on her lower lip suggestively. "We should do something about that," she whispers. Her hand wraps around my thick length before I can reply, and I close my eyes and let my head fall back as she rubs me slowly.

"Xanth," I whisper, unsure if it sounds anything like I mean it to. She continues, gripping me tighter and moving faster. "We can't," I manage to squeeze out. "Stop." She immediately releases me, and my body sags in relief, "I'm sorry," I mutter. "We can't complicate things."

She gives a stiff nod, her brows furrowing. Then she steps from the shower without a word, grabbing a towel and heading back into the bedroom. "Xanth," I call after her, "let's talk."

"Now, you want to talk," she calls back, adding a cold laugh. "Sure."

"It doesn't have to make things weird," I say, turning off the shower and getting out. There's no towel since she took it, so I go into the bedroom naked. She isn't there, and I groan, marching to the conjoining door and opening it. She's naked, drying her skin vigorously. My eyes linger on her backside, and my cock strains harder. "You haven't changed," I say. "You still refuse to stick around to hear me out."

She scoffs, wrapping the towel around herself. "You're dripping on my floor."

"I want to," I say, and she arches a brow. "Have sex," I add. "Fuck, I've dreamt about that moment so many times."

"Bullshit," she snaps. "You had me right there and you turned me down."

"Because things are messy right now, don't you think?"

She removes the towel, throwing it at me. I catch it, groaning as she bends to pick up a shirt. My cock begs me to take her, but I can't mess this up. "Donnie is screwing trying to find you," I snap. "In his eyes, you're still a thing."

"I told him it was over," she snaps, pulling the shirt on but leaving the buttons open.

"Fasten it," I growl, but she ignores me, dropping down onto the bed and not bothering to cover up. I keep my eyes fixed to her face. "And I . . ." I groan. "I have unfinished business back in Nottingham."

She stares at me with confusion. "You said you were single."

"I am, sort of."

"Sort of?"

"It's complicated."

She scowls, standing and fastening the shirt. She then grabs her leggings and begins to pull them on, leaving out any sort of underwear. When she pushes her foot into her trainer, I realise she's planning to leave. "What are you doing?" I demand.

"Going home."

"You're not safe there."

"I'll work it out."

"Work what out? Xanthe, when he realises you're back, he's going to take you to his place and keep you there. He was so angry earlier when he realised you weren't home."

"I'll call the police."

"They can't help."

She growls, stamping her foot in frustration. "There are laws," she cries, "and they're there to protect women from men like him."

I take her wrists gently. "I know," I say, trying to gain eye contact. "I get it, you're mad, but if you leave here, it'll end badly, and I won't be able to help you without killing all of them." She stills, letting my words sink in. "It's not that I don't want you, Xanth. Fuck, I want you so badly, it's painful. But the timing is wrong. You've dealt with a lot of shit these last few days, and your head is all over the place. If I took advantage of that now, it would make me selfish, and I'm trying not to be that with you."

She chews on her lower lip again, and I feel her relax slightly. Her eyes find mine, and she gives a brief nod. "Okay."

"You'll stay?" I ask, and she nods. I smile, pulling her into my arms. "Thank you."

"On one condition." I stiffen again, waiting for her demand. "Tell me the truth about Nottingham. Who are you running from?"

When I release her, she steps back with a steely glare in her eyes. She won't let this go. "Who says I'm running?" I ask, shrugging. I secure the towel around my waist.

"I know you too well. Who is she?"

I sigh heavily and sit on her bed. "Joanne," I mutter.

She scoffs. "I knew there would be someone," she says accusingly. "Why weren't you honest?"

"I didn't lie," I argue.

"Only you forgot to tell me about Joanne?"

"It's not what it seems. She left me, so we're not together." She eyes me suspiciously, and I shrug again. "What can I say? She chose better. They always do."

Xanthe lowers beside me. "That's not true, Reese. You're a good man."

I smirk. "Really? That's not what your body language said when you found out what I was doing for Donnie."

She shifts uncomfortably. "It was a shock. I'm a nurse. I save lives, not take them."

I feel a pang of guilt. She's new to all this, and I hate that she's been so exposed. "Jo was never truly mine to begin with. She's with my old president."

She winces. "Aren't there rules on that sort of thing?"

I laugh, but it's cold. "Let's just say I'm lucky to be alive. But it doesn't change the fact that she loves him and not me so . . . here I am, licking my wounds."

"I'm sorry," she mutters, placing her hand over mine. "Love hurts."

"It ain't the first time, and it won't be the last," I say, forcing a brightness to my voice. She doesn't miss the dig, and I divert my eyes to the ground. "I'm over it. She's happier without me there."

"You loved her?" she asks, but it's more like a statement.

"I've only ever loved once, Xanth. Maybe that was half the problem. I knew she wouldn't leave him, and I didn't want her to. No one after you could ever compare."

"You're not being fair," she whispers. "I didn't send you away."

More guilt engulfs me. It's not like she knew what her parents did. She couldn't have stopped it even if she had. But I've spent so long blaming them all, letting the bitterness seep into my exposed wounds, that it's hard to change my mindset. Maybe it was to protect me. Perhaps it still is. "We should get some rest."

I stand, pulling the sheets back and waiting for her to climb in. "I don't want to be alone," she says, slipping beneath the covers.

"I'm right next door."

Sadness fills her eyes. "You hate me so much that you can't even stay?" She grabs my hand. "Please."

I give a slight nod, and she smiles. "Let me put some shorts on," I add, going back into my room. I pull on the shorts and a T-shirt before going back and climbing into bed beside her. She lifts my arm and lies against my chest, tugging my arm around her shoulders. My heart swells, and I resist the urge to bury my nose into her hair and inhale her scent. Instead, I lie back and stare up at the ceiling.

If Donnie could see me now, he'd torture me for sure. He was so angry when he realised she wasn't home, and even when we suggested maybe she'd met a friend or was just simply busy, he refused to relax, insisting his men start searching for her. He's in way deeper than I realised, and he's not going to settle until he has her back in his clutches.

Xanthe

We lie awake in silence. Something is playing on Fury's mind, but he clearly doesn't want to talk. And he certainly doesn't want to fuck again. He made that perfectly clear.

I roll over, turning my back to him and closing my eyes. It's only seconds before I feel him slip from the bed and sneak back to his own room. I press my face into the pillow, allowing myself to feel mortified. He must think I'm a nutter, forcing him to lay with me. I groan, praying the next few days aren't awkward between us. The sooner I can get back to my life, the better.

The following morning, I wake and shower before dressing. I stare at the conjoining door with anticipation. I don't know anyone else well enough to feel comfortable just heading downstairs, but my inner bitch needs coffee desperately. I take a deep breath and tug the door open, only to find the room empty.

"Great," I mutter, slamming it closed again.

I spin to the other door when there's a light tap and almost cry in relief when Lexi sticks her head in and smiles. "Morning. I was wondering if you were awake or not. Bet you're starving?"

"I need caffeine," I admit, and she laughs.

"Follow me."

Downstairs, she pauses at the kitchen door. I can already hear voices from inside. "Just a warning, it's like a zoo in there. You have to fight for food and scream to be heard." She pushes the door open, and I stare wide-eyed at the chaos before me. "I tried to warn you," she adds, grinning before slipping her arm in mine and leading me farther into the lion's den.

Some of the men stop what they're doing to look at me. I feel myself blush under their intense stares. And then I spot Fury glaring at me, holding two plates of food. He closes the gap between us. "I was bringing you food," he says.

"Don't be ridiculous. She can't hide away in that room all day," says Lexi, taking one plate of food and handing it to me.

I offer a weak smile before she pulls me in the direction of the table. "Move up," she orders one of the bikers, who slides along the bench to make room for me. I lower, unsure how I feel meeting all these strangers in one go. It's overwhelming.

Lexi sits beside me, and I'm squashed between her and the biker who is now smirking down at me with a glint in his eye.

"Nyx," he says confidently, holding a huge hand out for me to take.

I place my plate down before running my sweaty hand down my shirt and taking his. "Xanthe."

This makes him grin wider, and he looks back at Fury, who I assume is still rooted to the spot behind me. "This is Xanthe?"

Lexi leans over me, slapping our joined hands until he releases me. She narrows her eyes. "Don't even think about it," she says, her tone warning, then she smiles at me. "Axel is the President and my old man," she says, pointing to the hulk of a man to the left of her, heading up the table. He winks, and I almost melt in a flustered puddle. "That's Grizz, the Vice President," she adds, pointing to the man beside him who's holding an adorable little girl. "And little Ivy, his daughter. Remember Luna?" she asks, and I nod. "They're her family."

"Never mind the taken men," says one of the bikers, leaning around Nyx. "What about the rest of us?"

Lexi laughs. "That's Ink," she explains, and he holds out a hand for me to shake, which I do.

"If you want me to show you around," he begins but stops when a shadow falls over us. I glance back to see Fury towering over me.

"Move up," he orders, and Nyx grumbles before shifting farther along and making room. Fury sits beside me, placing his plate down. "She doesn't need you to show her around," he says coldly. "She won't be here that long."

It's like a bucket of ice being thrown over me, and my appetite shrinks away. Lexi offers a small smile before grabbing a coffee pot and topping up a mug for me. "Here, wash away that bitterness with this," she says, glaring at Fury.

"Eat," he says to me, staring down at his own plate.

"I'm not hungry," I mutter, pushing my plate away.

He narrows his eyes before pushing it back in front of me. "Eat, Xanth. I haven't seen you eat properly yet."

His pushiness annoys me, and I move the plate once again. "I'll eat when I'm hungry," I say firmly.

He finally looks me in the eyes, and for a second, that lost look makes an appearance before he shuts it down. He doesn't understand why I'm angry. *Fuck, I don't either!* I just know I'm pissed with him. Maybe it's his rejection that stings, or the fact he clearly doesn't want me to know any of his brothers, like he doesn't want me to get too settled in his life. I take a sip of coffee, shaking my head in annoyance.

Fury's mobile rings, and I hear him sigh as he checks the caller ID. He presses it to his ear. "Yeah?" After a few seconds, he adds, "Of course. I've got church first, then I'll come." He disconnects and looks to Axel, who nods and then gives a loud whistle until the rest of the room falls silent.

"Church," he orders, and the men leave the room like scurrying ants. Axel leans over to Lexi, placing a lingering kiss on her lips before following. Fury is still beside me, staring at his hands resting on the table. Eventually, he stands, and although I feel like he wants to say something, he chooses not to. He leaves, and I release a long breath as Lexi gives me another small smile.

"Are you okay?" I nod, and she rubs my hand. "He's intense," she says, and it's as if her words press something inside me, opening the floodgates. The last few days suddenly catch up and tears pour down my cheeks uncontrollably.

An older woman rushes over with a box of tissues. Lexi pulls a few out and presses them into my hands. "It's okay," she reassures me as I wipe hurriedly at my wet face. The last thing I want is for Fury to come back in and see me like this.

"It's like a curse," says one of the women from across the table. "The Chaos Demons curse."

"What is?" asks Luna, taking a seat closer. The other

women follow suit, all shifting up the table, which only makes me feel worse, like some kind of zoo freak.

"They always manage to make a woman cry. Like they're slowly breaking us down until we're a mess, and then they swoop in and make it all better."

Luna grins. "Gemma, there's no way you've ever broken, not even for Fletch."

"Xanthe, meet Gemma, Duchess, Tessa, Jennie, and Foxy," Lexi introduces.

My eyes linger on Jennie, and I see recognition in her expression but I don't mention we've met. My attention goes to Foxy. She looks different somehow, more tired yet more dolled up. It's only eight a.m. and she's got a face full of makeup and is dressed in the skimpiest outfit. As if she senses my question, she smiles. "I'm a club whore." I gasp, and she laughs. "It's what they call us girls who hang around to satisfy their every whim." I don't mention that I already know, in case I'm forced to explain how Fury referred to Jennie.

"Only the single men," Lexi cuts in. "And we don't refer to them as whores, even though Foxy doesn't mind. The men refer to the single women as club girls or club bunnies. If you hear them say whore, you have my permission to hit them upside the head."

Duchess smirks. "Lexi is changing the ways of The Chaos Demons. Equal rights for all, even the whores." Lexi's head whips in her direction, and she laughs harder, holding up her hands in defence. "I'm kidding. But I'm old school, and I like the old ways."

"Well, the old ways aren't exactly PC, so we'll stick to the new ways."

"We're going off topic," Luna points out, but I was relieved they weren't focussed on me, and it's given me time to get myself together.

I sniffle and force a smile. "I'm fine. I don't know what came over me."

"The curse," says Gemma pointedly.

"He dismissed you whilst claiming you," says Luna. "It's confusing."

I shake my head. "He's just a friend."

"You're not friends," says Tessa, biting into a cold pancake and wincing before dropping it back on the plate. Her words confirm how Fury is making me feel, and I nod in agreement until she adds, "You're way past that."

"He's just helping me out." I feel Lexi's eyes on me as I spout the same crap I did last night. I groan, scrubbing my hands over my face. What have I got to lose by talking to these women who clearly have experience dealing with men who are as cold as they are hot? "Fine, I fancy him like crazy," I admit, "but he's not into me like that."

"Finally," says Lexi, smirking.

"He's so into you like that," adds Luna with confidence.

"Seriously, he isn't," I say. "He's giving me so many mixed signals, it's driving me insane."

"Let me guess, he doesn't want anyone else around you, but he doesn't want to be around you either?" Gemma guesses, and I nod. "It's because he's crazy about you."

"You're wrong," I say, "because I basically offered myself to him on a plate last night, and he couldn't wait to get away." My cheeks burn with embarrassment. "He snuck out my bed the second he thought I was asleep."

"It means nothing," says Lexi. "Just that he's battling with his own demons."

"Have you already done the deed?" asks Jennie, and I shift uncomfortably.

I nod. "One time. We haven't talked about it since, and he's acting like it didn't happen."

"He scratched the itch," she says simply, and Luna nudges

her. "What? It's true. He got what intrigued him, and now, he doesn't want her."

"Jesus, Jennie," snaps Luna, "do you have to be so blunt?"

"It's fine," I mutter, knowing her reaction is coming from a place of jealousy.

"See, a girl after my own heart," she says, rising to her feet, but her smile is far from friendly as she heads out the kitchen. "Excuse me, ladies, but I have to be ready when they need me. Church can be stressful."

"Don't mind her," says Lexi. "She's quite new to the club."

"She's right, though," I say.

"She isn't," Duchess cuts in. "And no offence, Foxy," she adds, "but don't take the advice of the club girls. If they knew a biker's mind, they'd be old ladies."

Foxy laughs. "Good point."

"He'll see what's in front of him," Luna reassures me.

I scoff. "Well, I won't be waiting around to see the end result. The second I can, I'm leaving here." They all exchange a knowing look, and I throw my arms up in exasperation. "I am," I reassure them. *Because I am.* If Reese Northman wants to deny his feelings, he can do it when I'm not here to witness it.

CHAPTER 11

Fury

Chevy sighs heavily before sticking a cigarette in his mouth and lighting it. The orange flame illuminates the inside of the car, and I roll my eyes, wondering where Donnie found such an amateur. If Xanthe was hiding out in the house we're watching, she'd have spotted that for sure.

"I have a gut feeling about this," he murmurs, releasing a lungful of smoke.

"Yeah? How come?"

"She came here a few times when I was following her," he says thoughtfully, and I narrow my eyes.

"You were following her? Why?" My heart rate picks up while I wait for his answer. Chevy is the type of guy to watch a room and hear every little secret, just so he can sit on it until he needs to use it for his advantage.

"The boss had me following her every move before they met," he confesses, and I almost breathe a sigh of relief, knowing he hasn't seen us together.

"Does he usually get so invested in a woman?" I ask casually.

He smirks. "You have no idea."

"What is it about her?"

"Man, you saw her, right?" he asks, laughing. "She's fine." I clench my fists at my sides. I don't like him talking about my Xanthe like that. "The fact she held out on him," he sniggers, "just made her more appealing. The man wanted to know what she was hiding in that tight little cunt of hers."

I push the car door open and get out, slamming it hard. I take a few deep breaths to calm the racing adrenaline inside me then head towards the house.

I hear Chevy call after me, but I can't stop or I might go back there and smash his head into the steering wheel. Instead, I raise my boot and slam it against the door, which pops open with little to no effort. It swings back, smacking the wall behind it, and I step inside. Seconds later, Chevy is behind me. "Fuck, man, this ain't staking it out," he hisses.

"I got bored," I reply, turning on the light.

The living room is bathed in the golden light, and a man sits upright, shading his eyes. "Jesus," he mutters, having clearly just woken up. "What the hell's going on?" He's wearing doctor's scrubs, and I immediately wonder why Xanthe spent time here.

"Where's Xanthe?" I bark.

He frowns. "Who the hell are you?" I grab his top and haul him to his feet. His terrified and confused eyes meet mine, and he gulps. "I don't know where she is."

"Call her," says Chevy from beside me.

"I deleted her number," he says. "She hates me."

"Why?" I find myself asking.

He almost smirks. "Cos I shagged her friend."

I shove him back onto the couch. "You two were a thing?"

He shrugs. "She was into me more than I was her."

"For how long?" It's way more than I need to know, and I

feel Chevy's eyes on me, questioning why I need this information.

"A few months."

I grab his ID card off the table, checking the name and committing it to memory before throwing it back down. "Forget we were here," I say, "or we'll come back, David Chapman, and slit your throat."

I head out with Chevy at my heels. "What the fuck was that?" he demands, and I wonder if he's pissed I took the lead for once or if it's because I went rogue without his permission.

I turn on him as we get to the car and shove him up against it. "Just because I'm compliant doesn't mean I can't fucking break your neck. I'm here because I always clear my debts, but your constant tone is fucking me off. You wanna find this bitch and sitting in a car for hours ain't gonna work for me." I release him and get in, slamming the door. "I need to fight," I add. "Take me to the club."

By the time we stop at Donnie's underground place, I'm itching to break something. My fingers tingle with anticipation the second we step inside to the cheers of the baying crowd. My shoulders instantly relax, and the tension leaves me.

I spot Donnie by the changing room. He's got a woman pressed against the door, and it doesn't take a genius to see she doesn't want to be there. I head over. "Boss," I say in his ear, and he stills. I make eye contact with the woman and see she's terrified. "She wasn't there."

"How do you know?" he spits, turning to face me. The woman sees her opportunity and rushes away.

"We went in."

He narrows his eyes. "You did what?"

"I don't have time to sit and wait," I snap. "If you want her, we're gonna have to kick down doors to get to her."

He thinks over my words, and then a slow, sly smile

spreads across his face. He pats my shoulder. "You're not as dumb as you look."

I force a smile even though I want to hit him square in the face. "I need a fight," I tell him. "One I'm winning," I add, so there's not room for arguments.

He gives a nod and indicates for his fixer to come over. "Find my man a fight. Not a fixed one. Let's see what he's got."

I roll my eyes as I head for the changing room. *I'll show the fucker what I can do.*

∽

I LEAVE THE RING FEELING A LOT BETTER THAN WHEN I ENTERED it. And even though Donnie's fixer clearly tried to screw me over with a much larger opponent, he still couldn't beat me.

I watch through swollen eyes as the bookie reluctantly counts out my winnings. Then I turn to Donnie and push the wedge of cash into his chest. He frowns, taking it. "Towards my debt," I say, heading for the door.

As my bike slows to a stop, I hear the music from inside the clubhouse. My body aches, just like it always does when I fight without warming up properly, and all I really want is Xanthe. But when I step inside, I see she's already occupied with some of the other brothers. She catches my eyes and smiles, but I don't return it, instead heading for the bar and taking a bottle of whiskey.

"Hard shift?" asks Axel, assessing me from his seat at the bar. I sit beside him, unscrewing the cap and topping up his glass before drinking directly from the bottle.

I slam it down and sigh heavily. "I needed to feel," I mutter.

"Did it work?"

I glance back to where Ink is whispering into Xanthe's ear and roll my eyes. "What do you think?"

"There's no cure," he states. "Coop will tell yah."

Coop looks up from his glass. "Huh?"

"For love, there's no cure," clarifies Axel.

Coop grins, shaking his head. "It can destroy your soul if you let it, Pres."

"Is that why you stayed single after Widow?" asks Axel.

He shakes his head. "Nah, I chose to put everything into Lexi. I didn't want her turning out like me or Widow."

"Did you stay celibate?" I ask, frowning.

He laughs. "Don't be crazy. I just didn't let them close enough to rob my heart." He takes a drink before adding, "It's different for you."

"How so?" I ask.

"You don't have kids."

"It's not kids he's protecting," says Axel, downing his drink in one then tapping my bottle for a refill. "It's his heart."

I scoff, filling his glass. "You make me sound like a pussy."

"I'm just speaking the truth."

I grab my bottle and stand. "Look at her," I say, "glowing in all their attention." The words sound bitter as I watch her laughing at something Hawk says. "Is it any wonder?"

"All you have to do is walk over there and claim her."

"So she can throw it in my face?" I ask, shaking my head. "I'm no good at it, Pres. Relationships just fuck up without me even trying."

"So, you stopped trying altogether?"

"It's easier this way."

"You keep telling yourself that, Fury, but I reckon we both know the truth."

I head for the stairs, stopping when a tiny hand grips my wrist. I turn to find Jennie, and my heart sinks with disappointment. "You want company?" she asks, smiling wide.

I give a stiff nod, and she slips her hand in mine, letting me lead her to my room.

Xanthe

I LOOK OVER TO THE BAR, AND MY HEART SINKS WHEN I REALISE Fury isn't there. I excuse myself from the guys who have spent the last hour trying to outdo one another to impress me. And if my head wasn't so full of him, maybe I'd have noticed, or even cared enough to entertain it.

I take the stairs two at a time. If I'm not mistaken, he'd been fighting, because even though I was across the room from him, I thought his eyes looked swollen.

I go into my room and grab my bag. I always carry a first aid kit no matter what, and I smile to myself as I head for Fury's room. I've spent the day without him, and I've missed him. At least I have an excuse to sit with him for a while.

I knock lightly and push the conjoining door open, stopping in my tracks when I spot Jennie, naked and dancing around the room to Beyoncé. Fury is watching from his half-sitting position on the bed, a bottle of whiskey in his hand.

She spins, her eyes falling on me, and her step falters. Fury then looks to me, and there's a hint of regret in his eyes which is quickly replaced with a confident smirk. "You coming to join us?" he asks, arching a brow, and Jennie gives a smug grin.

I scoff before slamming the door closed. *Pig.*

Minutes later, I'm on my bed staring out the window when the door opens. Fury clears his throat, but I don't acknowledge him, relieved I already have my back to him. *I don't even know why I'm so mad. He's single, after all.*

"She's gone," he says, and I want to retort with something smart, but I remain quiet, hoping he'll assume I'm asleep and leave. "It was a bad idea. I don't even want anyone else. I just saw you with them and . . ." He trails off. "I was jealous."

I narrow my eyes before looking back over my shoulder, unable to keep quiet any longer. "Fuck you."

He arches a surprised brow. "You're mad at me?"

"I'm confused by you," I snap, pushing to sit up. "You don't want me, but you don't want anyone else to want me either. So, fuck you, Reese Northman."

He shrugs. "You're right," he admits simply, stepping farther into the room. "I don't want to see my brothers pawing at you like some cheap whore."

My eyes widen. "Get the fuck out," I yell.

He realises his mistake and tries to backtrack, but I'm already off the bed and storming towards him. "I didn't mean it like that."

"Out," I scream, pointing to the door.

"I meant that's how they'll treat you."

"Maybe I want them to," I say, folding my arms over my chest. "Maybe having one of your big, strong brothers throw me around the room, treating me like a sexy whore, is exactly what I want." I narrow my eyes further, noting how his fists are clenched by his sides in anger. "Maybe," I continue, thrilled that I'm pushing his buttons, "I should sign up to be a club whore. Jennie can show me the ropes."

He charges me, sweeping me into his arms and kissing me with so much force, I almost lose my balance despite him holding me. I relax into his hold as his tongue sweeps into my mouth, sending flutters to my core. I gently cup his face, using the tips of my fingers to graze his jawline, and he groans somewhere deep in the back of his throat as he walks me backwards until my legs hit the bed. He lowers me down onto the mattress, crawling over me without breaking the kiss.

His hand strokes up my thigh, taking my skirt with it and allowing the cool air to calm my clammy skin. He pulls back slightly, his lips just a breath from mine as his hand pushes into my underwear. "You still drive me crazy," he murmurs, brushing his finger over my swollen clit. "And you're wet," he whispers, smirking as he lands another gentle kiss to my lips. I jerk as he rubs small circles over my sensitive area before pushing his finger into me. I arch my back from the bed, my eyes fluttering closed. "And if Lexi heard you say club whore, she'd be pissed," he adds, kissing along my jaw and down my throat.

The question escapes me before I can stop it. "Have you ever slept with any of them?"

He manages to shut me up with another toe-curling kiss. "Xanth, we're not about to discuss each other's conquests when I have my fingers inside you," he says, hooking his finger slightly to stroke that sweet spot inside. I shudder, my hands clinging to his shoulders. I need him so badly, and when I pull him down for another kiss, he rolls onto his back, taking me with him. I know without a doubt that he's not handing over control here as I mount him. Even when he was younger, he was commanding and assertive, telling me exactly what he wanted me to do.

"This needs to go," he says, tugging at my shirt. I grin, making quick work of unfastening the buttons despite my shaking hands. I pull it off and stare down at him, waiting for his next order. "The skirt can stay," he adds, lifting it slightly and taking hold of my lace thong. He tugs it hard, snapping it from me like it's nothing but paper then throwing it to the floor. "Better." I smirk, rubbing myself against him. The denim of his jeans presses right where I need him to be, and I moan out loud, shuddering. "Still need to be thrown around the bedroom?" he asks, arching a brow.

"I got your attention, didn't I?"

He lifts my skirt again, this time watching as I rub myself against him. His erection adds to the friction as I move faster. "I wanna see you come over my jeans," he murmurs, his eyes hooded and his breathing hitched. "Soak me." I moan, letting his words affect me. I grab handfuls of his shirt as the pulsating warmth rips through me at lightning speed. I have no control as my body jerks and my breaths leave me in short, sharp bursts.

"Fuck, you're stunning," he murmurs, gripping my waist and rolling us again so I'm back beneath him. He pushes to stand, and I feel the loss immediately, the cold air wrapping around me and calming my racing heart. He undresses quickly, his cock springing free as he shoves his jeans down his hips and steps from them. Once he's naked, he holds up a condom he'd retrieved from his back pocket, and I push the intrusive thoughts away that remind me he probably put that there for the club girl.

I watch as he rips the packet and sheaths his impressive length. He rubs the head of his cock up and down my entrance, gathering wetness before slowly pushing into me. Inch by inch, he opens me up, and I gasp, enjoying the feel of his size. Fury hisses, squeezing his eyes closed before pausing to allow us both to adapt to the delicious feeling. He rests his forehead against mine, finally opening his eyes. One is almost swollen shut, and I gently cup his face, adding a gentle kiss just underneath it. Oddly, I find him sexier bruised and battered.

"This is where I belong," he whispers. "Where I've always belonged." I nod in agreement, unable to find the words, and he slowly withdraws his length, looking me in the eyes as he slams back in hard enough to move me up the bed. "Are you ready for me, Xanth?" he asks, nipping my bottom lip. I nod, and he grins. "The last time we fucked in a bed, I had zero experience outside of you." He slams in a second time, and I groan with pleasure. He slides his hand down my thigh, resting it under my knee and carefully raising my leg, hooking it over his shoulder. "Now, I'm all grown," he adds with a smirk, slowing his movements so I feel every inch of him sliding into me again.

He glances down at our connection, watching as he disappears. He growls before picking up his pace, his movements jerky with each thrust. The intense build-up of a second orgasm happens immediately, and I'm so not ready for it as it tingles through me, hanging me on the edge of bliss. He presses his thumb to my swollen clit, and I cry out, falling over the edge, much to his delight.

I'm still panting when he pulls from me and taps my thigh. "Turn over and get that backside in the air," he instructs, and I do it without question. His hand pushes between my legs, and I jerk as he gathers my wetness on his fingers. I hear him licking them, humming his approval before he says, "You taste good."

I close my eyes, dropping my forehead to rest on my forearms while keeping my ass in the air for his pleasure. He pushes back into me, his cock filling me up. This time, there are no sexy words falling from his mouth as he fucks me, taking whatever he wants while grunting in pleasure. And I let him, because the sounds he's making turn me on so much. I want to be the only woman to ever make him feel like this. From now on, I'm claiming Reese Northman. *He's mine.*

CHAPTER 12

Fury

I don't think I've ever come so hard. Not since the first time I had sex, and that was once again with Xanthe. She snuggles into my side, our breathing heavy with exertion. "Let's do that again," I murmur sleepily, "in a few hours."

She giggles, and the sound warms my heart. "Last night, you couldn't escape fast enough, and now, you want to stay in my bed?" Her tone is teasing.

"You wouldn't take no for an answer," I say, smirking, and she lightly taps my chest in warning. "And as usual, you got your own way." That's not a lie. Xanthe always gets her own way because I have no defences when it comes to her. She breaks them all.

"It's not my fault you let jealousy win."

I shift onto my side, propping my head on my hand so I can look at her. "In all seriousness, stay away from my brothers." My tone leaves no room for teasing, and her smile fades. "The punishment for fighting my brothers over a woman that

I haven't claimed is serious. But I'd go there, Xanth, for you." I stroke my fingers down her cheek. "Don't make me."

She gives a small nod, not quite meeting my eyes. "I wouldn't want to cause you any problems with your family . . . again."

"Now, sleep," I say, flopping back down and wrapping my arms around her until she's snuggled against my chest.

～

THERE'S BANGING, AND IT WAKES ME FROM A PEACEFUL SLUMBER. I sit upright, taking a second to realise I'm not in my own room. Xanthe stirs beside me, and for the first time in years, I relax knowing she's here and I didn't dream the entire thing. The banging sounds again, and I carefully slip from the bed, trying not to disturb her.

Grizz is pacing outside the room, and I frown, wondering why the hell he's knocking on Xanthe's bedroom door. "I tried your door first," he explains, answering my unasked question. "You have a visitor," he adds. "Donnie."

My frown deepens. "What the fuck is he doing here?"

"He's acting all smiles and shit, but I reckon he suspects she's here. So, if I were you, I'd hide her just in case," he says, nodding past me to Xanthe.

I glance back, relieved to see she's still sleeping. "Tell him I'm not here," I snap, pissed that Donnie would come to my home. He's overstepping boundaries.

"I don't think that's a good idea."

I groan in frustration. "Fine. Let me wake her and explain."

"I'll tell him you're on your way. Grab a whore on your way so it throws him off the scent."

I close the door, locking it to be safe, and go back to where Xanthe is looking peaceful. I bend down to place a kiss on her cheek, and she smiles, stretching out until the sheet falls away. I stare at her naked body, my cock arousing at the sight. "Good morning," she murmurs, her voice raspy from sleep.

"We have a problem," I say, and I hate the way her smile immediately fades. "Donnie has turned up here. He's downstairs."

She sits up, grabbing the sheet and holding it to her chest. "Shit. Does he know I'm here?"

"I have no idea. I'm gonna go and find out. But for now, you need to stay in here."

I go to leave, but she grabs my wrist, halting me. "What if he knows and he hurts you?" There's genuine concern in her eyes, and I smile, rubbing my thumb over her lips before leaning down to capture her mouth in a kiss.

When I pull back, I offer a reassuring smile. "I can handle him. Don't worry, I'll be back."

I knock on Jennie's bedroom door, and it's minutes before she opens up, rubbing her eyes sleepily. One of the prospects is asleep in the bed behind her. "Grab something sexy," I order, and she perks up immediately. "Nothing like that," I add quickly. "I need you to play a part. Follow my lead and don't mention Xanthe." She nods, grabbing her silk nightdress from the floor and pulling it on while following me downstairs.

Donnie is waiting patiently by the bar with Axel. I hear the brothers in the kitchen, the usual breakfast banter ongoing, although I know they'll be waiting for a signal in case this shit goes downhill.

"Donnie," I greet, keeping hold of Jennie's hand.

He makes a tsking sound, smirking slightly as his eyes run over my bruised face. "You came off worse than normal." His eyes then run over Jennie, and his smirk gets bigger. "But you found a good way to forget the pain."

"Don't let the bruises fool you, I only get hit when I want to."

He chuckles. "I called. You didn't answer."

I shrug. "I slept well." I glance to Jennie, and she returns my smirk. "After our workout, I took tablets to knock me out." He stares at me for a few silent seconds, but I don't break eye contact. He's checking my body language to see if I'm nervous. "Was it urgent?" I ask.

He shrugs. "Not particularly. I sent Chevy instead. I wanted you to watch the hospital." Axel scoffs, shaking his head in irritation, and it gains Donnie's attention. "Something you want to say?"

"We agreed you'd make use of Fury to pay his debt. Wasting his time watching out for some bitch you're lusting after don't seem like a good use of his time."

Donnie laughs. "You're right, Axel. And I respect you, so I'm going to take your remark on board."

"I'm pretty sure the debt is almost paid," Axel adds, arching a brow.

Donnie's smirk fades. His jaw clenches, and he shoves his hands in his pockets. He's annoyed. "It's paid when I say it is."

It's Axel's turn to laugh. "That's where you're wrong," he says firmly. "This is my club, Donnie, and the only reason you're still breathing is because I allow it."

I clear my throat, and they both look in my direction. "Is there a reason you're here, Donnie?" I ask, breaking the tension.

His smile returns. "I'm glad you asked. I have a fight. If you win, it will clear your debt completely."

Hope fills my chest. With him out of my life, things will be easier. "Okay."

"Wait," says Axel, concern filling his face. "With who?"

Donnie grins wide. "See, he has sense," he tells me, nodding. "Always ask who your opponent is."

"Cut the crap," snaps Axel. "Who is it?"

"It's a surprise."

"Bullshit," Axel growls. "He ain't fighting a big fight without knowing who it's with."

"It's fine," I say. "I'll win."

"Excellent. See you tomorrow, eight sharp. You'll be in the ring by nine." And he leaves.

Axel glares at me. "What?" I ask. "I'll do the stupid fight, and we can get him out of my life."

"There's no way he's gonna make it that easy to get out of debt."

"You don't think I can win?" I ask, smirking.

"It depends who you're fighting and you know it."

∼

I FIND XANTHE IN THE SHOWER AND STRIP QUICKLY TO JOIN HER. She gasps when I run my hands over her soapy body, sliding my palms up to her breasts and teasing her nipples while gently nipping her neck. She turns in my arms. "What happened?"

I kiss her, running my fingers through her wet hair. "He just wanted to line up a new fight."

"Is that wise?" she asks, skimming her fingers over my swollen undereye.

"I'll be fine," I reassure her. "And once I win this, I'm debt free."

"That's why you fight for him?" she asks, frowning. "And why you do the things you do?" I kiss her again, but this time, she pulls back. "Stop avoiding the conversation."

"Yes," I reply. "I was supposed to throw a fight before and I didn't."

"Why?"

I shrug. "I don't like to lose."

"Isn't it illegal to throw a fight?"

I laugh. "After all the shit you've seen, you're concerned he's fixing fights?"

She smiles. "I want you to be done with him."

"After tomorrow night, I will be."

"And then what?"

I sigh, pressing my forehead to hers. "I don't know. He's got someone watching the hospital for you today."

"He knows my shift patterns."

"He isn't giving up, that's for sure."

"Maybe I could change my job," she suggests. "We could move?"

"Move?" I feel like I'm finally settling here, and there's no way I can go back to Nottingham. "There aren't too many fractions to this club," I say, "and I like this one."

"I don't see how I can stay here when he's looking for me. And I don't want us to lose one another again." She stands on her tiptoes to kiss me. I'm relieved she feels the same way, because the thought of losing her again is too painful to imagine.

"If I make you mine," I begin, unsure how she'll take the news, "the club will have no choice but to protect you."

Her eyes widen. "What does that mean?"

"I could make you my old lady."

Her brows furrow. "Old lady?"

I back her to the tiles and lift her, lining myself up at her entrance and kissing her until she's breathless. As I enter her, I add, "It's basically like marriage. I'll belong to you, and you'll belong to me. You'll be my old lady."

She gasps as I fill her. "Marriage without the big ceremony?" she whispers, her eyes tightly closed as I fuck her.

"Yeah, but just as binding."

"It's not legal though?"

I move faster, and she cries out, gripping my shoulders. "It is in my eyes and in the eyes of the club." I feel nervous as I wait for her answer. It's huge. I've never even considered taking an old lady. But this way, I can make sure she's protected. No matter what happens to me, she'll always be looked after. She tightens around my cock, and I see her begin to spiral, so I slow down. Her eyes shoot open questionably. "I want your answer," I say, taking her lower lip between my teeth and gently tugging it.

"I can't even think straight," she pants.

I slam into her, and she cries out again. I grin. "I can draw this out as long as needed."

"Fine," she hisses, narrowing her eyes. "Whatever you want."

Relief floods me, and I move fast, fucking her so hard, my legs cramp in protest. She shudders, screaming out as her orgasm rips through her. I follow, releasing into her on a long, drawn-out groan. I rest my forehead on her shoulder, waiting for the blood to drain from my cock and fill the rest of my body again.

I pull from her, and she glances down. "You didn't use a condom?"

I frown slightly. I always use protection, *but it felt right.* "I guess I got carried away."

She shoves against my chest. "You dick."

"What's the issue? You've just agreed to be my old lady."

She gets out the shower, wrapping a towel around her body. I rinse off, watching as anger radiates from her. I don't understand why she's so mad—I can't think of anything better than filling her with my babies.

"That's not real life, Reese. There's no security in pretending to be your fucking wife." I don't like the way she curses at me, and I narrow my eyes as she sits on the toilet and uses tissue paper to wipe herself.

"It's real," I snap. "Real as any marriage."

She scoffs. "Right, so when we split and I'm left with your kid, I can take you for half of everything, can I?"

I turn the shower off and grab my own towel, wrapping it around my waist and storming into the bedroom, shaking my head in anger. "First of all, I'd never leave you if you had my kid. Secondly, you're my old lady, I'm not going anywhere, and neither are you."

"We fucked twice," she yells, staring at me in disbelief. "Don't you think it's a bit soon to make promises like that? And it's definitely too soon to have a baby. You've lost your mind."

The second she steps into the room, I rush her, shoving her against the wall and caging her in with a hand either side of her head. "I love you." I say it clearly, and she inhales sharply. "I've loved you since the second I saw you in those ridiculous pink trainers with your hair sprayed up within an inch of its life."

"It was a nineties party," she whispers defensively.

"I never stopped. You're it for me, Xanthe. So, if you're telling me I'm not the one for you, I'll back off while you try to figure that out. But you're my old lady, so get to the same page as me real quick or things will get awkward." And then I kiss her hard before heading back to my own room.

Xanthe

I STARE AFTER HIM, MY HEART HAMMERING HARD IN MY CHEST. He didn't even give me a chance to tell him I love him too. That no man since him has ever made me feel like he does. But my heart is begging me to be cautious because Fury has the power to destroy me.

I dress and decide to go explore. If Fury is really taking me as his old lady, I should get to know this place and the people in it.

I head downstairs, taking a deep breath before pushing myself to walk into the large main room, where there's a sea of bikers. I've never been one to shy away, but I feel intimidated in this room full of big, burly men. I'm relieved when I see Lexi heading towards me with a wide smile. "Hey, great to see you out of your room," she says brightly. "We wondered if Fury had grounded you after seeing you with Nyx and the others."

I return her smile. "No, but he wasn't happy."

She links arms with me and leads me over to the couches where some of the other women are sitting. "Well, rumour has it he's close to claiming you."

I shrug. "He mentioned it, but I don't know how serious he is, and to be honest, I don't really know what the entire claiming thing entails."

"We can definitely help you with that," she says, and we sit down. The other women are having smaller conversations amongst themselves, so I turn slightly to Lexi. "It's basically like marriage," she tells me.

"That's what Fury said."

"It's pretty huge when the guys take an old lady, and it doesn't usually happen more than once in a biker's life. If he's chosen a woman to be his old lady, he's letting his brothers know that he intends to be with her for the rest of his life."

"But it's not legally binding or anything, so there's nothing to stop us separating or him changing his mind."

"He won't change his mind," she says, almost laughing. "The fact he even said those words to you means he's already in love with you."

I scoff, even though deep down I feel the same. "It's been a few weeks since I met him again."

"You've known him for years, Xanthe. Maybe the love never left him."

I nod in agreement. "I know how he feels."

"So, why is it so hard to believe he's committing to you?"

"He mentioned that I'd be protected by the club." She nods. "What if he's only doing it for that reason? I know he cares about me. He doesn't want Donnie to hurt me."

"You're at the clubhouse in hiding, which means the club is already protecting you. But if you're worried, talk to him."

I nod. "What about duties?" I ask.

She arches a brow. "Duties?"

"Yeah, do I have to do anything with this special role betrothed to me?"

She laughs. "Just be his wife."

"Without the paperwork," I cut in.

"Look, if marriage means so much to you, then make it legal. But you don't need to. Fury will protect you and love you and do everything a committed man does."

"What about the other side of it?" I ask. "The not so legal part?"

"There's no point pretending it's not there because we all know it is. But they do everything in their power to keep us out of it. The only time I know shit's gone down is when my man returns to our bed covered in blood. I've learned to not ask questions because I never get answers. All he ever needs from me is comfort."

"I don't know if I can live with not knowing that side of his life. But then, at the same time, I don't think I want to know."

"If you knew it all and the police came knocking, you might slip up. Not knowing is for the best. Besides, from what I do know, these guys rid the world of bad people, and I'm okay with that."

CHAPTER 13

Fury

I sit by the bar, my eyes fixed on Xanthe chatting with the other old ladies. "She fits right in," says Coop, taking the seat beside me.

"Like she was always meant to be," agrees Axel from my other side.

I grin. "I'm gonna make her my old lady," I tell them.

"Good man," says Coop, slapping me on the back in congratulations.

"I just wanna get this fight out the way before I make it official," I add.

"It would make things easier for her if she's got our protection," says Axel. "It's the right move."

"She's not so sure," I admit. "I mentioned it to her last night. I think she feels like I'm rushing into it."

"It has only been a few weeks," Coop agrees, "but when you know, you know, right?"

I nod in agreement. "She'll come round. I've given her a

little space, but once this fight is done and we make it official, she'll realise I'm serious about her."

When she came to bed last night, she seemed a little more settled. And although we didn't talk about it anymore, she didn't protest when I slipped into bed with her, or when I gave her another orgasm before we fell asleep wrapped around one another.

But today, she seems distant again, and I've hardly seen her between her helping Duchess in the kitchen and then Luna in the garden. I'd have preferred to spend the day in bed worshipping her before this fight.

I stand. "I have to go and get this out the way."

"Me and Grizz will be there," says Axel, shaking my hand. "And I'll keep the brothers on standby in case."

"It's just a fight," I reassure him. "Nothing's going down tonight."

I head over to Xanthe, and she looks up, smiling. I lean closer and kiss her. "I have to go."

She gently places her hand on my arm. "I have a bad feeling about this," she mutters.

I brush some hair from her face. "I love you. I'll be back in a few hours." I add another chaste kiss and head out. All these doubters are making me anxious.

~

THE FIGHT CLUB IS PACKED OUT, EVEN MORE SO THAN USUAL. I head straight for the changing room and strip down to my shorts. When Chevy comes in minutes later, he doesn't quite meet my eyes, and before I can question him, Donnie comes in. He grins. "You ready, champ?" The way he addresses me concerns me some more. He doesn't usually come back here before a fight.

"Why do I feel like this is a big deal?" I ask warily.

"Isn't every fight?" he asks, smirking.

"No," I say bluntly. "There's something going on."

"There're rules to this fight," he says, arching a brow.

I shake my head, knowing I won't like what he's about to say. "I'm not throwing the fight," I snap.

"Nothing like that. It's a fight until knockout."

"What?"

"Years ago, it would be a fight to the death, but apparently, they're banned . . . but you get the idea." I know that look—he means death.

I swallow the lump in my throat. "No."

"No?" he repeats.

"I'm not killing anyone in that ring."

He laughs. "Let's not be dramatic. I didn't say those words, did I?"

"But you meant them." *Fuck.* I knew he was bloodthirsty, and I've gotten rid of bodies belonging to fighters, but I assumed it was from fights that had gone wrong.

"I don't think you understand me, Fury," he says firmly, stepping closer. "I have a room full of rich and important men out there tonight. They're wanting a real fight. Like the good old days."

"Axel won't allow this," I snap. "He'll be here any minute, and you really don't want a war with the club."

This makes him laugh, and he pats Chevy on the back, who forces a smile. "He's so confident I'm afraid of his precious club," he scoffs, then he straightens up and his smile disappears. "I know you have her." His words settle in my brain, but not quick enough for me to admit or deny it before he continues. "I know she's your childhood sweetheart." I swallow down a response. "Get in the ring. Fight like you agreed, and you get to walk away debt-free and with the girl."

"And if I lose?" I ask, my heart slamming hard in my chest.

His lip lifts slightly at the corner, giving him a more

sinister look. "But I thought you said you won't." And then he turns and leaves.

Chevy shifts uncomfortably. "Who am I fighting?" I ask.

He shrugs. "I don't know, but I don't think it's gonna be good. He's keeping it to himself."

"Fuck," I hiss.

"And just a heads up, he ain't letting any bikers in tonight."

"Are you fucking kidding me?"

He shakes his head. "Look, man, I like you, and I hate this. If I was you, I'd back out."

"How can I?" I snap. "No. I've got to go through with this." I sigh. "Look, I'm asking a lot, but get a message to Axel for me." He hesitates, but before he can refuse, I add, "Just tell him, if this goes wrong, she's my old lady." He gives a stiff nod and leaves.

I pace the room, trying to keep my shit together. And when the knock comes on my door, I square my shoulders and take a deep breath. I'm a good fighter, and so far, I've only ever lost one fight. I can do this. *For Xanthe.*

I go out to the beat of a song I've never heard. Usually, I choose my own music for big events, but there's nothing usual about any of this. I keep my head lowered as I climb into the ring. It's not until I look up into the eyes of my opponent that the rest of the room fades away. I can hear my rapid breaths and the fast pace of my heart as the crowds fade to nothing. Ripper stares back, almost smirking. He bounces on the spot, warming his muscles and readying himself for the slaughter that's about to happen. He tips his neck from side to side and gives me a wink. He's been waiting for this for months, and fuck knows I deserve it.

The bell sounds, bringing me from my daze. I'm still rooted to the spot, and Ripper takes full advantage, closing the space between us and slamming his fist into my nose. The blood vessels burst immediately, spraying us both. "It's good to see you, *brother*," he spits before jabbing my stomach fast and hard. I wince, trying to shake it off and gain control of the situation, but my mind is reeling, and I keep scanning the crowd for *her*. As if he senses it, he grins, pulling me in close so his mouth is to my ear. "She got rid of it," he hisses, bringing his knee up as he forces me down, making contact with my stomach again. This time, I go down, coughing violently.

He doesn't give me a second to recover before he's on me, pinning me down so he can climb over me. I lie on my back, and he stares down at me with a smirk. "Come on, it's no fun when you don't fight back. Give the crowd a show." He proceeds to pummel my face, and then the bell rings. He doesn't stop immediately, giving me an extra few hits before climbing from me and going to his corner.

I pull myself up, and the sound of the crowd booing hits me. I wince, pushing to my feet and going to my corner. Chevy hands me a bottle of water, and I take it, rinsing my bloody mouth and spitting into the offered bucket. "What the fuck was that?" yells Donnie, marching over.

"Fuck you," I hiss, grabbing my towel and wiping my nose. "You did this on purpose."

"You better start fighting," he warns, "cos if you don't, I'm gonna get her back and give her a night she'll never fucking forget. Am. I. Clear?" he bellows.

The next round is as brutal as the first. Letting Ripper get so many shots in the first round has put him at an advantage, and even though I manage a few moves, I don't execute them in the way I usually would.

Round three is better. I manage to break his nose and possibly his cheekbone. I just need to hit him one good time to knock him out, and then maybe this madness can stop.

When the bell sounds for round four, I'm feeling more like myself. This fucker isn't even a brother anymore. He'd made that perfectly clear when he asked Axel's permission to end me. I owe him nothing.

I slam my fist into his face, hitting the same cheek with two quick jabs. He stumbles back, and I follow up with a round kick, which makes him lose his balance and he crashes to the floor. I dive on top of him, straddling his waist and punching him over and over. The crowd is going wild, and then I hear her calling to me. I glance to my left, and there she is, with tears streaming down her face. *Joanne.* "Please," she begs. "Don't."

It's not lost on me just how much she looks like Xanthe. Maybe that was the reason I was so attracted to her. But it was never love, and that's the reason Ripper could never forgive me. I fucked his old lady . . . I got her pregnant when he couldn't . . . and it wasn't even about love.

Joanne's distraction gives him enough time to shove me back, and I realise he must have been holding back before, because now, as he lands each precise blow, I feel as though my skull is breaking. The crowd is cheering, they're so fucking fickle, and I pray for the bell to ring. But as he pins my hands under his knees and continues to rain down blows, I know it's not going to sound.

This was always Donnie's plan. This way, he wins.

Xanthe

The atmosphere has changed around the room, and the bikers are quiet. Even the women have felt it and have asked several times what's wrong. It's not until Axel storms in, followed quickly by Grizz, that I realise it might be something to do with Fury. "Motherfuckers," Axel yells, kicking a wooden chair that flies across the room and breaks against the wall.

"What's the plan?" asks Fletch.

"I don't have a fucking plan," Axel shouts angrily. "My plan was to monitor the situation from inside, but that stupid fucker made sure we didn't get in."

"How bad is this gonna get?" asks Coop cautiously.

The men exchange a look I don't understand, and I push to my feet. "What's going on?" My voice comes out less confident than I wanted it to, and Axel stares at me with a mixture of worry and pity.

He looks away. "Lexi, get her out of here. Get all the women out."

I feel her gently tug my arm, but I shrug her off, frowning. If this is about Fury, I have a right to know. "Where is he?" I demand. "Has something happened to Fury?"

"Church," he barks, heading for their sacred room, which Fury made very clear women weren't allowed to enter.

The men file into the room and then the door slams shut. I turn to Lexi, who offers a pitying smile. "I'm sure he'll fill you in when he can."

"That's not good enough," I cry. "Something's very wrong, I can feel it," I add, rushing after them and shoving the door to church open. My breathing comes out in fast bursts as the men all turn to look at me. Axel stands, his large frame looking scarier than usual as he grips the edge of the table. "I need to know if he's okay."

"You can't be in here," says one of the bikers, trying to guide me from the room.

"If you don't tell me what's going on, I'll go and find out for myself," I threaten, looking Axel in the eyes.

He scrubs a hand over his brow. "I don't know if he's okay," he admits. "I don't know fuck all because Donnie wouldn't let us in. But I'm guessing it's not good."

I let his words sink in, pain searing my heart. I almost fall to my knees as the realisation of what he's saying hits me. The biker who was pushing me out is now gripping me to keep me upright. "I'll come find you when I know more," Axel says. "Try not to worry. He could be fine, and I might be overthinking this." But we both know he isn't.

The biker leads me from the room, but I pull free of his supporting arms and head out. I need air because I feel like the walls are closing in on me. Shoving the door hard, I inhale the cool evening air. *Fuck.* I knew something bad would happen. I had a dread in the pit of my stomach all day. What if Donnie knows I'm here? What if the fight went bad? I pace back and forth, not leaving the safety of the doorway, just in case.

A movement catches my eye, and I glance up in time to see a cat running across the carpark. And then my eyes land on a dark heap in the gateway. I can't see what it is, but it doesn't look like it belongs in the centre of the driveway. I take a few steps closer. "Hello?" There's no movement or sound. I look around, but there's no one else here, so I go closer. It's only when I'm a few steps away that I realise it's a person because I see a hand splayed out to the side. "Shit," I mutter, dropping down beside the body. My nursing instincts kick in, and I gently place my hand to their shoulder. "Hi, I'm a nurse, are you hur . . ." My words trail off as the hood falls away and I'm faced with Fury. "Oh shit," I gasp, falling back onto my arse and covering my mouth so I don't scream. His face is a bloody mess. His eyes are completely swollen shut, and his lips are bloody and busted. His nose is broken, and he's covered in small cuts.

"Reese," I cry, scrambling to my knees and unzipping his hoody. I run my hands over his chest and feel wetness there. When I bring my hands up, they're soaked in blood. "Help," I scream. "Somebody help!" Seconds later, Lexi appears in the doorway. "Get Axel," I yell. "It's Fury!" I lean down to check his breathing.

The men run out, and Axel reaches me first, skidding to a stop beside us. "Holy shit, is he breathing?"

I nod. "Barely."

"We need to get him inside," says Grizz, looking around cautiously.

"We can't move him," I cry, wiping my tears on the back of my hand. I lean my ear back to his nose and mouth to monitor his breathing. My fingers dig into his wrist, feeling a faint pulse. "Call an ambulance."

"We have to get him inside," Grizz says again, more forcefully this time. "They could be watching. We're targets out here in the open."

"He's right," says Axel, touching my shoulder.

I take a few deep breaths, trying to calm my racing heart. "Okay, but we need to move him really carefully and slowly. I don't know if there's damage anywhere else."

The men gather round, each taking a part of Fury under my orders and lifting with a trained precision I've only ever known from soldiers.

Once inside, he's laid on the floor. In the light of the room, his injuries look so much worse, and I fight my tears to try to assess him while Grizz calls for the ambulance.

I get the men to help me carefully roll him into the recovery position, placing cushions behind him to keep him there, and then I feel down his spine. Nothing feels out of place, but without a scan, I can't be sure. I keep my finger on his pulse and my ear to his mouth. "Please be okay," I whisper. "I love you."

When the ambulance arrives, they jump into action, and I stand back, Lexi holding me as we watch them hook him up to their monitors. They eventually get him stable enough to move him, and they place him on a spinal board before putting him onto the trolley.

"Is anyone coming in the ambulance?" the paramedic asks.

"Me," I say, stepping forward.

"No," says Axel firmly. "I'll go."

"But—"

"It's too risky," he cuts in. "Donnie will be waiting for you there. I'll keep you updated."

I stare helplessly as he heads out after them. Lexi gently squeezes my arm. "He'll be fine."

"You don't know that," I mutter. "He was in a bad way."

"Try and stay positive."

"I'm a nurse," I say, "I know a dying man when I see one." A sob escapes me, and I clamp my hands over my mouth. "Oh god, what if he dies and I'm not with him?"

"He knows you love him, Xanthe," says Luna.

"It's not enough," I cry. "I should be with him, holding his hand, begging him to stay with me."

"He's a Chaos Demon," says Gemma simply. "He'll fight with everything he has to be back here with you."

I don't bother to reply, instead heading upstairs to my room. Once inside, I break down, huge sobs racking my body. I can't get the image of his battered face out of my mind. I go to the bathroom and scrub his blood from my hands. Then I strip from my clothes and pull on the T-shirt he wore last, pressing the soft cotton to my nose and inhaling his musky aftershave. I crawl into bed, lying on his side and soaking his pillow with my tears.

~

I wake with a start to find Lexi shaking me. "Wake up," she whispers. "Axel is on the phone." I sit up, grabbing the offered mobile and pressing it to my ear.

"Yes?"

"He's stable," he says. "It took them some time to get him there, but for now, he's stable. He's got some swelling on the brain. If that doesn't settle soon, they're talking about a . . . fuck knows what it's called, but they wanna remove a part of his skull."

"Ventriculostomy," I tell him as fear grips me. "I want to come and see him, Axel. He needs me."

"I told you, it's not safe. I won't leave him, and I'll update you."

"Do you know what happened yet? Who he had a fight with?"

"No, but I have men looking into it."

"Have the police been informed?" I know the hospital would have to call the police to report an assault. It's standard practise.

"Yes, but I can't tell them anything," he says in a lowered voice.

"Like fuck you can't," I snap, and Lexi gently rubs my arm as if to calm me. "He could die. You have to tell them everything, including how Donnie is looking for me. Fury was only trying to protect me."

"We'll talk when I get back."

"You just promised not to leave him," I remind him.

"And I won't. But at some point, I have to update my guys, so a prospect will come and take over from me for a while."

I hand the mobile back to Lexi, and she turns her back, talking in whispers before disconnecting. "He's in the best place," she says, sitting beside me.

"I have to see him," I cry. "What if he dies and I never get to see him again?"

"You heard Axel, it's not safe. Donnie will be waiting for you."

"I don't care," I say, throwing the sheets back. "He can take me, just as long as I see Fury first."

"And then what?" she asks, standing. She looks pissed, and I keep my sarcasm to myself. "Fury asked the club to keep you safe if anything bad happened. If you take yourself off to the hospital and Donnie gets to you, Axel will then have to worry about you. He's got enough on his plate already."

Guilt swamps me, and I give a slight nod. "You're right. Sorry."

She sits back beside me. "I know this is hard. I can't imagine how you feel. But you need to listen to Axel. He's just doing what Fury asked him to do."

"What if I call my mum? She loves Fury too, and she could go and see him. It's not like Donnie knows who she is."

"I'll ask Axel."

～

When Axel returns later that evening, there is no change and the doctors have decided to drill a hole into Fury's skull to allow space for his brain to swell. But before he goes into church, Axel gives me permission to call my mum.

I don't waste any time, and the second she answers, I burst into tears. She waits patiently, even though I can tell by her voice that she's worried. And when I finally get it together, I blurt it out. "Fury is in hospital."

"Oh my lord, are you with him now? I'll come right away."

"I'm not there, Mum. I can't be there because . . ." I sigh. "Everything is such a mess."

"I assumed things were going well. You texted to say you were really happy."

"They're fine between Fury and me," I tell her. "Mum, there's an ex who's being stalkerish. And the thing is, I think he's kind of the reason Fury is in hospital. I think he fixed one of his fights."

"You're in danger?" she asks, sounding panicked.

"I'm staying at Fury's club with his friends. Yah know, the ones he told you about?"

"The biker place?"

"Yeah, and they're really nice. They'll keep me safe, but it means I can't go sit with Fury right now. I was wondering if you would go for me and keep me updated?"

"I already have my shoes on," she says, and I smile.

"It's really important you don't tell anyone that you know me, or that Fury and I have history."

"If anyone asks, I'll tell them I'm his foster parent. That's the truth."

I relax a little. "Thanks, Mum. I love you."

"I love you too. I'll call you when I can."

CHAPTER 14

Fury
Two weeks later

The pain is searing through my head like a hot poker. It's so bad, I want to rip open my own skull just to relieve it. But I can't move. *Why the fuck can't I move?* I try to open my eyes, but it feels like they're grainy and swollen. My mouth is dry, and even when I try to lick my lips, there's nothing much there.

"He's waking up." It sounds like Axel. *What's he doing here?* "Brother, you had us all fucking worried," he says, and I feel his hand on my shoulder. "Nurse," he calls. "He's waking up." *Waking up? Nurse?* Nothing is making sense.

A gentle hand feels my forehead. "Mr. Northman, I'm a nurse. You're in Royal London Hospital. You've been in the wars, and we've had to keep a very close eye on you," she says gently. "Can you open your eyes for me?" I try, *I really do*, but they won't budge. It's like they're glued shut. "Okay, can you squeeze my hand if you can hear me?" She places her cold fingers into my hand, and I squeeze. It's not much but enough for her to feel it. *Why do my arms feel so weak?*

"Perfect. Well done. Don't worry too much, things will start to make sense. I'll grab some eye drops to see if that helps," she says as she releases my hand.

"Fuck, man, we thought you were gonna die," says Axel. "What the fuck happened?" *Good question.* "I'm gonna call Lex. Everyone will be pleased to know you're waking up. This last fortnight took its toll on us all, especially Xanth."

Xanth? Who the fuck is Xanth? I only know one Xanthe, and I haven't seen her for years.

Xanthe

Relief floods me when Axel calls to tell us Fury is awake. I've spent the last two weeks in agony, desperate to see him, to hold him, and to tell him how much I love him. The closest I've gotten is when Mum visited him and placed the phone beside his ear. And we still have no answers. We don't know where Donnie is, and even though Axel is sure he's out of the country, he won't risk letting me go to the hospital. And we have no idea who Fury fought, but maybe now we'll get some answers and make them all pay.

It's not until an hour or so later, when Mum calls, that my heart sinks again.

"He's confused, and he still can't open his eyes," she tells me. "He isn't talking, but the doctor thinks it'll all come back to him over the next few days. He said we just need to keep talking to him and reassuring him. We won't know the full extent of the damage until he's fully awake and back with it."

"Is he hopeful he'll get all his functioning back?" Brain injuries are unpredictable, and it's hard to know what damage is done in the early stages.

"Sweetheart, you already know the answers," she says gently.

I nod, even though she can't see me, and sadness fills my heart. "I know, I just want some hope."

"The fact he's awake is hope," she says reassuringly.

"But the fact he hasn't opened his eyes yet isn't."

"It's been an hour," she says with a small laugh. "Let's give him time."

Time. I'm so sick of people saying that word. *It's not the right time for you to leave the clubhouse. In time, he'll be back to normal. Time is a great healer.* Everyone seems to have something to say to try to reassure me.

"Can you call me if he opens his eyes?" I ask.

Fury

TWO DAYS. TWO DAYS OF LISTENING TO PEOPLE TALK ALL AROUND me. Two days of not being able to see them, and two days of not being able to ask them what the fuck is going on. I had a fight, one I can't remember, but that's not unusual. I am a fighter, I know that, but what's confusing me is that I never lose.

And the second mystery is why my foster mum is here. I haven't seen or heard from her since they sent me away, and it's not like I'm a kid who needs parental supervision.

Axel keeps talking about Xanthe, and because of Dianna turning up, I know he means Xanthe from when I was a kid. But again, why the fuck is she around? Were they notified when I came into hospital?

And why is Axel here? Why am I in London? Where's Ripper? Where's Joanne?

So many questions and no way of asking.

∽

NICOLA JANE

It must be early. Axel isn't here, as he said goodbye some hours ago. He only ever leaves at night, and apparently, he leaves a prospect outside the door, much to the nurse's annoyance.

I take a deep breath and try to open my eyes. "Come on," I hiss to myself. "It's not rocket science."

"There he is." I relax immediately at the sound of Joanne's voice. I feel her hand on my cheek, and then she places a light kiss on my forehead. I open my eyes, just a little at first, but enough to let a light in that sends another searing pain to my head. I hiss, and her blurry outline appears to step back. "Oh baby, are you in pain?"

I try again, this time opening them a little more. I blink a few times, and she becomes clearer. She smiles, and I use the button the nurse placed in my hand to sit the bed up some more.

Jo perches on the edge, holding my hand. "We've been so worried," she whispers. "I haven't slept since the fight."

She's never missed any of my fights, even when she's had Ripper beside her. Her secret looks have always been enough to get me through. I look past her, and she must sense who I'm waiting for. She kisses my lips. "He's not here, baby." The fact she's here alone confuses me. He wouldn't let her leave the club without an escort—usually me—but as I'm laid up, surely, he would have sent a prospect at the very least.

"W-where?" I manage to croak out, frustrated I can't speak like normal.

"He's with Axel catching up. Listen, no one here knows about the fight yet, and I really want to keep it that way."

"F-fight?" I repeat. "Lost?"

She frowns. "You don't remember?" I give my head a slight shake.

The nurse comes in to check my vitals. She gives me a double take and smiles. "Well, ain't you a sight for sore eyes?" she asks in a teasing tone. She pulls out her pocket torch and flashes it in my eyes, causing more pain. I wince, and she apologises. "It's nice to see those baby blues."

Jo stands. "Erm, I don't think he can remember the fight," she says, and the nurse looks at me.

"Can you talk?"

I frown deeper, trying to think of the word. I feel like most of my words have left me, and the ones I want to say flit in and out of my mind before I get a chance to try and say them. "Little," I eventually say.

She gives me a reassuring smile. "It's quite normal for speech to take a while to return. The fact you can say some words is a great sign. And I'm afraid you might find your memory is patchy."

"Is it likely to return?" Jo asks.

"Maybe," says the nurse. "Maybe not. What's the last thing you remember?" she asks me.

I think hard. "Nottingham," I reply.

Jo looks worried. "He hasn't lived in Nottingham for months."

The machine beside me begins to beep loudly as my heart slams harder in my chest. Months? *Why the hell did I leave Nottingham?* The nurse silences the machine. "I think he's had enough visitors for today."

"I'm his wife," Jo snaps. "I want answers."

Xanthe

I DON'T LIKE THE NEW BIKER WHO'S TURNED UP AT THE clubhouse faking concern for Fury. Everyone else seems to love him and can't do enough for the guy. But there's something shifty in his eyes, and I don't like it.

Gemma sits beside me at the bar and follows my eyeline to Ripper. "What?" she asks.

"I didn't say anything."

"Your face is saying everything," she states. "You don't like him."

"I don't know him."

"So, why don't you like him?"

I smirk. She never misses a trick. "There's something off about him," I reply, shrugging.

"I thought the same."

We exchange a grin. "It's an air around him," I say, "arrogant yet nervous. He's hiding behind fake confidence."

"He's lying about something," she adds. "He's too shifty when he speaks, and he doesn't quite meet Axel's eye."

"Have you mentioned it to anyone?" I ask.

"By anyone, you mean Axel or Fletch?" She laughs. "No."

"Maybe you should."

"In case you didn't realise, they don't listen to us. As far as they're concerned, he's a brother."

"But surely your word might make them think it over, see things they might not have."

"Are you worried he's here to take your man back home?"

I scoff. "No. Fury wouldn't leave without me anyway," I say with false confidence. The truth is, not being able to see him has left me feeling a little lost. Without his reassurance, I don't know how he feels. We were only just starting out again and then this happened. "I really want to see him," I add. "I was thinking maybe I could go in my uniform. No one's going to be looking at a nurse."

She arches a brow. "Only your crazy ex who knows you work there, and he's the reason you're in hiding."

"We don't even know where he is," I exclaim. "The guys are busy. They wouldn't even know if we leave."

"I will have Fletch watch you all night if I have to," she warns. "Axel will tell you when the time is right."

I go upstairs in a huff. It's almost impossible to get out of here because there is always someone on the gate lately. And even when there isn't, there are brothers hanging around, and they all know I can't leave.

Fury

I HEAR AXEL FROM OUTSIDE THE ROOM BERATING THE NURSE FOR not calling him to tell her things had changed since he'd left. When he finally bursts in, I manage a smile, and relief floods his face. The nurse is hot on his heels, still trying to explain that she told my next of kin.

"I'm his fucking next of kin," he barks.

"The lady who was here earlier, she said she was his wife."

Axel's eyes narrow and he looks at me. Before I can attempt to talk, the nurse jumps in. "He's not managed to find his speech. These things take time."

"Jo," I manage to whisper.

"Jo?" he asks, and I nod. "What the hell was she doing here?" And then something passes over his face, but he doesn't bother to explain. Instead, he turns to the nurse. "She isn't his wife. They aren't together. Don't let her in here again."

"Actually, it's not up to you," the nurse says, turning to look at me. "It's up to you who visits. Can she come in here?" I nod, and she smiles smugly before leaving.

Axel glares at me. "What the fuck is going on, Fury?"

"I-I don't . . ." I take a breath. "Memory." I know the sentence is wrong, but the words won't come, so Axel sits beside me in the chair.

"You can't remember?" he asks, and I nod. "But you remember Jo isn't yours, right? She chose him in the end." When he sees my confusion, he sighs. "You left Nottingham to come here because everything came out, Fury. Ripper found out about the two of you."

I close my eyes and think back to Jo and the promise she made me. *"I'll tell him, and we can be together. A family of three."* I was shocked when the pregnancy test came back positive, but I was ready to step up and own up. I hadn't meant to start fucking around with my former president's wife, but she was unhappy. Ripper didn't want to have kids, and Jo found it hard. She wanted her own little family. We connected unintentionally—I was around when she needed to talk, and things progressed. I certainly didn't mean to get her pregnant, but she was over the moon. How could I tell her it wasn't what I wanted?

I picture Ripper leaning in close to my ear. *"She got rid of it."* My frown deepens. I don't know if that's a real memory or a dream.

I didn't ask Jo about the baby, but it's only just come back to me, and I feel that tightening in my chest again. The machine beside me bleeps, and Axel rolls his eyes before turning the sound off. "Relax. It's gonna be a lot to process, but we don't need little miss nurse bitch turning up to kick me out."

The door opens, and Axel groans when a nurse enters. She's wearing a face covering. "What the fuck are you doing here?" he snaps, and she removes the face mask.

"I had to see him," she hisses. And then her eyes fall to me and she smiles wide, rushing over and throwing her arms around me. "I've been so worried about you," she cries.

I glance at Axel, who looks pissed. "How the hell did you even get out of the clubhouse?"

Clubhouse? She's from the club? The nurse pulls back and runs a hand down my cheek before kissing me gently on the lips. I frown. I mean, she's hot, don't get me wrong, but Jo would slam her to the ground for touching what's hers. "I love you," she whispers, her eyes teary.

I glance back to Axel again, my eyes wide with confusion.

Axel sighs, rubbing a hand over his forehead. "Xanthe, he doesn't remember."

Xanthe. *This is Xanthe?* Shit, she's grown. Of course, she is, it's been years. I smile a little, but she looks horrified. "Xanthe," I manage to say.

"Yes, it's me," she says, smiling again. "See, he does remember," she shoots to Axel.

"Do you?" Axel demands.

"Xanthe," I say again. "First . . . love."

"Yes, that's right," she cries again, swiping tears from her eyes. "And your last, I hope," she adds, giving a nervous laugh.

My smile fades, and Axel shakes his head slightly in disappointment. "He doesn't remember, Xanthe. He remembers what you had before."

My head hurts from everyone around me talking in riddles.

Xanthe

I SEE IT IN HIS EXPRESSION. *He doesn't remember me*. The way he keeps looking to Axel for confirmation is one of the many signs he doesn't have a clue about the promise he made me. "What do you remember?" I ask.

"N-Nottingham," he replies.

"Okay, but we can fix it. I can update you, and we can get back on track," I say, my voice wavering slightly. This is not the big reunion I had planned.

The door opens, and a woman comes in. She looks from me to Axel and then to Fury. "What's going on?" she asks, staring pointedly at me. I remember my uniform and snap out of the current terror I'm feeling.

"Who are you?" I ask politely.

"His wife," she says firmly.

I inhale sharply, and my heart twists painfully. "Not strictly true," snaps Axel. *Strictly? Why isn't he saying it's not true at all?*

She steps in front of me, effectively pushing me to step back, and places a gentle kiss on Fury's head. He looks pleased to see her, relieved even, and he takes her hand. I stare at the connection, wondering how many lies he's told.

"I should . . . erm," I look back at the door, "go."

"Don't go," says Axel. "Not on your own, anyway."

"I just . . . I need to . . . oh god." I rush from the room, unable to hold it together.

Annabella looks up from behind the desk. "Xanthe, what are you doing here?" she asks, jumping from her seat and rushing to me while looking around suspiciously. My supervisor places an arm around me protectively. I'd told her Donnie was stalking me. How else would I explain not being in work for weeks?

"I came to see my . . . friend."

"Hottie in room two?" she asks with a grin. "Wow."

"How is he?" I ask. "Like really?"

"He's doing good. He's showing improvement every day, and once he can get up and walk, the doctor will release him."

"Really? That soon?"

"Well, apart from his memory, there's no lasting damage. He's very lucky. The neurologist will have him come back in a few weeks to see how he is. You know what brain injuries are like—he'll need monitoring for any permanent changes."

Axel steps from the room, and Annabella gives my arm a gentle squeeze before she goes back to work.

I look through the window in the door. The woman is sitting on the bed showing Fury something on her mobile phone, and he's smiling.

"Who is she?" I ask.

"Jo."

"His ex?" I almost screech.

He nods, taking me by the arm. "We need to get you back to the clubhouse and then we'll talk."

By the time we get back, I feel sick. Fury talked about Jo, but he didn't mention she was his wife or that they were still a thing.

I follow Axel into his office, and Grizz joins us. "What's going on?" he asks, looking back and forth between us.

"He's fully awake," says Axel. "Eyes are open, and he's trying to put things back together in his head."

"That's great news," Grizz says.

"Jo turned up at the hospital," he adds.

Grizz frowns. "Why?"

"Because apparently she's his wife," I snap, dropping down onto the couch.

"They're not married," Axel tells me.

"Well, whatever you bikers call it," I mutter.

"She isn't his old lady either," he adds. "She's with Ripper."

My head shoots up. "What?"

"Which makes me wonder if Ripper knows his old lady is off visiting her fling?" asks Grizz.

"Yeah, it got me wondering too," Axel says in agreement.

"Wait, isn't that why he left Nottingham?"

"Yep," says Axel, popping the P. "So, why would he allow her to visit him?"

"Maybe he doesn't know," Grizz suggests.

"Or maybe she's trying to figure out what he knows," I say. They both turn to me, waiting for me to elaborate. "Well, Ripper was acting shifty when he was here," I explain.

"In what way?" Axel asks.

I shrug. "Just odd, like he was nervous."

"I didn't pick up on that," he replies.

"Gemma did," I say smugly, and his eyes narrow. "She agreed with me."

Axel sits down. "Okay, Miss Marple, what else have you got?"

"What if he's back for revenge? Maybe he knows more about the fight and he came to check what you know?"

Axel scoffs. "He wouldn't dare."

"Wait," Grizz cuts in. "She might have a point. You wouldn't let him end Fury when he asked. Maybe he came back to help him on his way after he heard he was in a bad way."

"He wanted to kill Fury?" I demand.

"He asked, I said no, hence why Fury came here. Shit happens, and Jo was half to blame. But Ripper wouldn't come here and do it under my nose."

"So, why is he here?" I ask. "If he hates Fury, he's not here out of concern."

Axel thinks, running his hands through his hair. "I don't know. I questioned it myself when he showed up. He just said he had business in the area. He didn't mention Fury, but when I told him, he looked genuinely surprised. Especially when I told him Fury lost the fight."

"Why is that a surprise?" I ask.

Axel laughs. "Cos he never loses."

"Maybe he lost on purpose," suggests Grizz.

"He wouldn't throw the fight. And until I can get hold of Donnie, or Fury's memory returns, I won't know the answer to that."

"What if he was fighting someone he thought he deserved to lose to?" Grizz pushes. "Like Ripper."

CHAPTER 15

Fury

"What do you remember today?" Jo pushes. It's the same question she asks me every evening when she turns up. I've noticed she always appears after the guys have left, almost like she's avoiding them. I shake my head, and relief floods her face.

"Ripper," I say simply. So far, I haven't challenged her on anything because I haven't had the energy . . . or the words. Panic crosses her face, but she relaxes again when I ask, "Where is . . . he?"

"He thinks I'm out shopping," she says with an uneasy smile. "He's sorting some business." *Shopping?* It's almost seven in the evening.

Something feels off. It's been days since I woke fully, and no one can answer anything. Jo is acting weird, and even Axel seems preoccupied. He asks me every day if Jo visited, how she seemed. The entire situation doesn't feel right, and I still don't have the energy or the words to have a full conversation about it. I'm frustrated, and it's starting to show. I sigh heavily and turn my head away.

The door swings open, and we both look over to see Xanthe stumble in. She looks up, flustered, with her arms full of bags. "Oh," she says when she spots Jo, "you're here."

Jo places her hand over mine. "Of course, I am. I'm his wife."

Something passes over Xanthe's face, and she squares her shoulders. "Well, I'm his oldest . . . friend."

"Funny, he never mentioned you," Jo states indignantly.

Xanthe ignores her, placing the bags on the table. "Mum's sorry she hasn't been these last few days," she says, opening one of the bags and pulling out a pack of my favourite biscuits. She holds them up with a grin. "She sent supplies, though. I told her the hospital feeds you, but you know what she's like, forever worrying." She begins unpacking the bags, and Jo watches through narrowed eyes.

Eventually, she picks out a pack of Percy Pig sweets. Jo rolls her eyes some more. "I don't think filling him with sugar is going to do him any good. And as a nurse, you should know that."

"A little of what you love won't hurt, especially when you've been through so much."

The door opens again, and another nurse walks in. "Visiting is over," she says, looking directly at Jo.

"What about her?" she asks, nodding at Xanthe.

"She's staff. Now, say your goodbyes, there's always tomorrow." I don't miss the wink she gives Xanthe before leaving.

Jo huffs, tipping my chin back and placing a lingering kiss on my lips. I have no doubt it's for Xanthe's benefit because she hasn't been affectionate the entire time I've been here.

Xanthe gives a sarcastic smile and a little wave as she leaves, rolling her eyes once she's gone. I have no idea why she hates Jo so much.

She approaches the bed, perching on the edge. "Axel told me you have short-term memory loss," she begins, and I give a nod. "So, what I'm about to tell you will confuse you, and I shouldn't really even say anything because the doctor said it could confuse you more if we overload you with information." She's blabbering, a sure sign she's nervous. I almost smile at how well I still know her, even after all this time. I have so many questions, but the words won't come, and then she continues.

"I love you, Fury." It's not the words I was expecting, and I frown. "And you love me," she adds. *I did.* I loved her a long time ago, but her parents saw an end to it. "You came into this hospital a few months ago. I was your nurse, and we became friends again." My head hurts, and the pain forces me to squeeze my eyes closed. "I know it's a lot," she rushes to add, "but I wouldn't lie to you, Reese." The use of my given name has me opening my eyes again. They stare into her sad blues, and my heart twists.

"I don't . . ." I trail off, shaking my head. I have no idea what she's talking about, and it doesn't matter how much I try, I still don't remember.

"I know you don't remember," she finishes for me with tears balancing on her lower lashes. "But I needed you to know that before all this, we were starting to plan a life together."

"Jo," I say, wanting to remind her that I have someone, even if she isn't completely mine.

"I don't know what happened between you," she says. "You never told me fully. But Axel said you and her split after Ripper found out about you." I inhale sharply, and the beeping of the machine beside me rings out. She rushes around the bed to silence it. "You need to stay calm," she mutters. *Easy for her to say.* "It all came out, and Axel made you come to London and stay at the club."

I shake my head again. If she's telling the truth, why

would Jo be here? There's no way he'd let her out of his sight if he knew everything. *"She got rid of it."* His words return to me, and this time, his sneering face appears in my mind, causing me to shudder.

"Leave," I whisper, turning my head away from her.

"No, Fury, please, I just need you to understand."

"Leave," I repeat, more forcefully this time. "I don't . . ." I take a breath, "know you." I turn to find her sobbing softly. "Leave."

Xanthe

I CRY ALL THE WAY BACK TO THE CLUBHOUSE, AND WHEN I GET inside, Axel is waiting for me, his face red with anger. "What the fuck did I say to you?" he bellows, causing some of the other bikers to turn to see what the commotion is.

"I had to see him," I cry. "He doesn't even remember we're a thing."

He pinches the bridge of his nose. "Tell me you didn't bombard him with information."

"It's not information. It's memories. It's our life."

He steps closer, pointing a finger in my face. "You were only in his fucking life a couple months."

"He still made me his old lady," I yell angrily while swiping tears from my cheeks.

"And how did he react to your trip down memory lane?" he demands. Thinking of the way Fury dismissed me makes my heart hurt, and I stare down at the ground. "Exactly how I thought," Axel adds. "The doctor told us we can't fill in his blanks. Filling his head with memories he doesn't have will set him back. You should know all this."

Lexi moves closer, placing an arm around my shoulder. "Let's go get a drink," she says softly, leading me towards the kitchen.

Duchess looks up, and the second she sees I'm upset, she pulls out a chair for me to sit, then grabs a bottle of something and some glasses. She places them on the table, and I spy the bottle of whiskey Axel was asking about earlier, accusing some of the brothers of taking it. Lexi smirks. "We always take one for emergencies. What he doesn't know won't hurt him."

I wipe my face on my sleeves as Duchess pours us each a finger of whiskey. "I just wanted to spark something in him," I whisper.

"And did it?" asks Lexi, handing me a glass.

I take it gratefully and drink some, closing my eyes as it burns my throat. "Nope. He asked me to leave."

"He was probably overwhelmed," Duchess suggests. "Once he's thought it over, he'll want to speak to you."

"What if he doesn't?" I whisper, my voice breaking slightly. "We've only just found one another again, and now, he doesn't even remember."

"Then you have to make him," says Lexi firmly.

"I tried that, and you saw how Axel reacted," I mutter miserably.

"Fuck Axel," she whispers in a hushed tone. "Soon, Fury will be home, and he'll need a nurse." She stares at me expectedly.

"Me?"

"Why not you?" she asks, shrugging.

"Because he sent me away, Lexi. I don't think he's gonna want me hanging around, especially now Jo's here."

Duchess scoffs. "Please, we all know you and Fury are meant to be, so, I agree, make him see you're his one."

∼

I LAY LOW FOR THE NEXT COUPLE DAYS. AXEL IS STILL PISSED, even though Lexi convinced him the idea of me nursing Fury back to health is a good one. And today is the day he's coming home. I'm not sure if I'm nervous because he rejected me or because I've got to nurse the man I love, knowing he doesn't remember that he feels the same.

Axel fills the doorway to my room "We need to talk," he says.

I sit up, bracing myself for more lectures. "I know I have to be professional," I begin.

"It's not that," he says before I can finish. "The men just voted on this, meaning I can tell you some stuff that's been happening." I sit straighter, eager to know what he has to tell me. "But it stays between us, Xanthe. The other women can't know. I don't like the women involved in all this shit." I nod in agreement.

Axel heads over to the window chair and sits. "We think you're right about Ripper."

"You do?"

"He's avoiding us. We've asked to meet, but he always says he's busy. That's not normal for a club. If your President wants to see you, you ask when."

"Do you think he knows more about the fight?"

"I think he was the one who fought Fury."

I gasp. "What?"

"He's the only one Fury would allow to beat him like he did. When Fury came to London, he was ashamed. Fucking around with a brother's old lady is not something a club can forgive."

"Yet you did?"

"Because of two things. One, I knew about Jo and her promiscuous ways. She wanted a kid, and she used Fury to get it."

My heart drops. "They have a child?"

He gives his head a shake, and I almost slump back in relief. "Ripper forced her to get rid of it."

"Oh. Shit. What a bastard."

"Number two, I don't like Ripper. He was voted in as the president there, but to be honest, he's just another in a line of bad ones. That part of the club isn't run by blood. Normally, I'd have a blood relation do that, or any kind of relation to a founder of The Chaos Demons, but I am the only blood relative. My father had great dreams of expanding, and I hate that I have to pull the plug on that."

"You're ending the Nottingham club?"

He gives a nod. "I was already making that decision, but Ripper's pushed it to happen sooner." He clears his throat. "We think he's using Jo to get to Fury."

"How?"

"It would cause alarm bells to ring if he was to show concern for the man he wanted to kill. It didn't happen in the ring as planned. It would explain why Jo has been allowed to turn up to visits without him. We think they're waiting for Fury to come here, then Jo will either do something or she'll get access to him for Ripper."

I process his words. "But you're going to stop her, right?"

"Fury believes she loves him. He thinks things are still great."

"Then tell him the truth."

"I want to, but you know what the doctor said about telling him everything. Since you blurted out your little part, he's not spoken to any of us. Not even Jo."

"Good," I mutter.

"She can't be left alone with him."

"She's coming here?" I snap, pushing to my feet. "Are you kidding me?"

"Once he's settled, I'll get rid of her. I also need to use her to lure Ripper here."

"How?" I shake my head. "Actually, don't tell me."

He stands and heads for the door. "What about Donnie?" I ask, and he pauses, giving me a sheepish look.

"We have him."

"Have him?" I repeat.

"I can't tell you that part."

I narrow my eyes. "How long have you had him?" He grins, marching out the room. I growl and chase after him. "Answer me."

"I can't. Club business."

We get downstairs. "Club business, my arse. If I find out you've had me hiding away here for no reason, I might hurt you," I threaten.

He laughs. "Look, I kept my promise to Fury. You're safe."

"He doesn't even remember," I hiss as the door opens and Nyx enters with Fury hooked on his arm.

I pause to stare at him. He looks frail and weak, nothing like the man who left me a few weeks ago, telling me he wouldn't be gone long. His eyes find mine, and for a fleeting second, I see something, recognition maybe. But he looks away as Jo comes in behind the pair, holding some bags. The prospects rush over to grab them, and she smiles gratefully.

A few brothers head over to help Nyx, and they lead Fury to the couch. I follow Axel, who stops by the couch. "Great to have you home, brother," he says. "I have you a fabulous nurse."

Fury looks at me again, but this time, he looks annoyed. Jo narrows her eyes and scoffs. "Not her."

"Can we have a word?" asks Axel calmly. She nods stiffly, following him towards the office. "And you, Xanthe," he adds to my surprise.

We get inside, and I close the door. Axel sits behind the desk, pointing to the seat in front of him for Jo, who sits. He tips his head to me, indicating I should go to him, which I do, much to her annoyance.

"We haven't had much time to catch up," he begins, "what with you avoiding me."

She flusters. "I haven't been avoiding you. I can't visit Fury in the daytime."

"Because of your old man?" asks Axel smugly.

"It's no big secret," she hisses.

"And what would he say if I told him you were visiting Fury?"

"Fury will go mad if you do that," she says with confidence.

Axel leans forward, resting his arms on the desk. "You know how I feel about my club," he says firmly. "I protect them with everything I have. The men are my family, as far as I'm concerned. My blood."

"If this is some big speech about how I'm getting in the way, save it. Fury loves me, and I'm here for him."

"What's the plan here?" he asks with a smirk. "Leave Ripper?"

"No. Yes. I don't know."

"I also love every single old lady under my protection," he says carefully, and I stand a little taller knowing he's referring to me in that. "My men pick their old ladies too wisely for me to doubt them, so when they choose, I back them one hundred percent."

"What are you talking about?" she snaps impatiently.

"Fury chose well," he says. She eyes us cautiously, waiting for him to continue. "He chose Xanthe."

Jo stands abruptly, causing the chair to scrape the floor loudly. "Bullshit."

"Just because he doesn't remember yet doesn't mean it didn't happen."

"Let me go ask him," she snaps. "Or show me her damn tattoo."

Axel stands too, towering over the desk. "Sit the fuck down," he bellows loudly, and she does so without question. "Don't disrespect me or Fury's old lady again." He takes a calming breath. "You have two options now—tell me what you know and I decide if you're innocent in all this and let you walk, or keep lying to my face and I kill you and your old man at the same time."

Jo begins to cry, and I stare at the floor. I might dislike her, but I don't want to see her upset. "Ripper is so angry," she sobs. "He refuses to let it go."

"Why is he back here?"

"To end Fury," she admits, and I stiffen at her confession.

"Xanthe, go check on Fury. Don't leave his side until I come find you." The command in his voice is strong, and I leave, knowing that arguing will only piss him off.

CHAPTER 16

Fury

I stare up at the bedroom ceiling, feeling more frustrated than ever. When the door opens and Xanthe walks in, I almost yell at her to leave, but the words don't seem to come, so instead, I mumble some kind of sound and give up, looking like a complete idiot.

"I bet you're glad to be home," she says, but there's caution to her movements, almost like she expects me to kick her out. When I still say nothing, she picks up the box of medication I've been sent home with and places it on the nearby bedside table. "It's normal to feel tired, and I'm sure being back here is taking it out of you, so feel free to get some rest. I'll just quietly monitor you." She can't be serious thinking she's sitting here watching me sleep, but she lowers into the recliner.

"No," I manage, and she sits straighter.

"Sorry?"

"No."

She pushes to her feet and moves closer. "Erm, no, you don't want to sleep?" I growl angrily, and she arches a brow. "I don't understand caveman." I almost smirk at her smart mouth, and she feels the mood lighten, taking it as a sign to sit on the edge of my bed. "I imagine you're feeling frustrated," she says, and I give a nod. "You never had any patience," she adds with a small smile. "The doctor said not to bombard you with information, that filling your head with memories might set you back and confuse you more."

I think over her words. It's the most anyone's told me so far, and it makes sense, so I force out, "Facts."

She looks pleased with this and nods. "Yes, I can tell you facts." She thinks for a minute then says, "Okay, you have serious head trauma from the fight you had. Your brain swelled so much that the doctors had to perform an emergency operation to remove some of your skull just to give it room." I nod, remembering some of this from the nurse telling me when I woke up. "The swelling went down, but there's some temporary damage. That's normal, and hopefully, your memory will return along with your words." I nod again, still staring at her expectantly. She thinks some more.

"We met again because of a previous fight," she explains with a laugh, and I find myself smiling too, like her happiness is infectious. "I was on shift, and the nurses were all whispering about a fit biker who showed up in emergency." She rolls her eyes in amusement. "I could hardly believe it when you walked into my room." Her eyes lower to where her hands rest in her lap, and she knots her fingers together, something I remember her doing as a teenager when she was upset. I place my hand over hers, and she looks up again, our eyes meeting for the briefest second before she forces an uncomfortable smile and pushes to her feet. She begins fussing with the sheets. "Of course, you insisted we have a coffee after my shift. You were hurt," she adds in a lower voice. "I didn't expect that."

"Hurt?" I repeat.

"You told me my parents were the reason you got sent away." My heart twists. I'd been angry, mainly with her parents but partly with Xanthe for making me love her in the first place. I never truly got over her, and now, as she stands before me looking upset and vulnerable, I feel that familiar urge to hold her. "I took you to dinner with my mum." I frown, hating that it's another thing I don't remember. "She explained what happened, and you forgave her, I think."

"Dianna," I say, and she smiles, nodding.

"Yes. And that's why she visited you at the hospital. I couldn't be with you because of the danger, so she went and let me talk to you on the phone whilst you were out of it."

I close my eyes. I remember dreaming about a woman speaking to me, telling me she loved me. When I open them again, Xanthe is back in the chair. "Fight?" I ask.

She looks hesitant before replying, "Yes, you went to a fight that was organised by Donnie." When I frown, she says, "You owed him money, and the fight was to cancel the debt." I don't like the sound of that, but she continues regardless. "Axel was supposed to come and support you to make sure Donnie didn't screw you over, but when he got there, he wasn't allowed in."

"I . . . I lost."

"Yes, you lost, which surprised us all. Apparently, you never lose." I grin, and she rolls her eyes, laughing. "Anyway, I found you out front. You were in a bad way."

"Here?"

"They must've dumped you here for Axel to deal with. I'm pretty sure they hoped you were dead."

"Why?"

She groans. "Fury, if I tell you everything, it won't do you any good, and Axel will kick me out of here."

"Please," I whisper, and she sighs.

"I was dating Donnie. You didn't approve and advised me

to break up with him. He didn't take no for an answer and became obsessed. You brought me here to the clubhouse to keep me safe."

It sounds like something I'd do. After all, I spent a long time loving Xanthe. "And with you owing money, you'd spent some time working for him, so you knew he was looking for me. You were coming up with a plan to keep me safe forever."

The door opens, and Axel enters with Jo behind him. She's been crying, and I immediately push to sit up, wincing through the pain in my head. I hold out my hand, and she rushes to me, allowing me to tug her against me. Xanthe stares at the ground while Axel rolls his eyes. "Xanthe, give us a minute, would you?" She doesn't need asking twice, rushing from the room.

Axel waits for the door to close before glaring at Jo. "Say what you need to. Make it quick."

Jo wipes her eyes even though there're no tears. "I terminated the baby," she announces, not meeting my eyes. I knew that. *Fuck knows how.* Maybe the fact she isn't showing and she's yet to mention it. "Ripper made me."

Axel steps forward again, and my attention goes to him. "Brother, I don't wanna set you back, but it's shit you gotta hear." I nod, and he looks relieved before motioning to Jo to continue.

"You fought Ripper in the ring," she mutters. "Donnie contacted him and told him you owed money. Ripper offered to put on a good show." *Donnie.* There's that name again. It proves that so far, Xanthe is the only one who's been upfront and willing to tell me shit.

"He . . . he found . . ." I sigh impatiently.

"Yes, he found out," she mutters. "He was angry, beat the crap out of us both," she says bitterly.

"And you decided to stay with him," Axel cuts in. "Get to the fucking point."

"He's my old man," she says, her eyes pleading with me to forgive her. And as I look at her, I realise that I feel nothing. I'm relieved she isn't having my baby, especially if she chose Ripper. I release her hand, and she begins to cry again.

"Jo is going home, back to Nottingham," Axel tells me.

"Ripper?" I ask.

Axel smirks. "She's getting the train back . . . alone."

There's a knock on the door, and Grizz enters. "You ready?" he asks Jo, and she nods, leaning down to place a gentle kiss on my cheek. "I'm sorry." A searing pain shoots through my skull, and I growl, gripping my head. I squeeze my eyes closed, and I see her . . . *Jo, she's ringside, begging me to stop. And there beneath me is Ripper, bloodied and battered. My fists are throbbing.*

"Fury?" Axel's voice brings me back to the present, and my eyes shoot open. They're all staring at me with concern.

Xanthe

It hurts way too much to watch the way he cares for her. How the fuck does he remember that but not us? It makes me question if any of it was real.

I crash into a hard chest, and strong hands steady me. Coop grins. "You lost in thought?"

Tears spring to my eyes, and he immediately holds me, allowing me to sob against his chest. "It's just temporary," he soothes. "All of this hurt and upset isn't forever."

"What if he never remembers?"

"How could he not?" he asks, sounding amused. "You two were meant for each other."

"Jo mentioned a tattoo." I sniffle, wiping my eyes and taking a step back. "She asked to see my tattoo to prove I was Fury's old lady. What did she mean?"

"It's standard that when a guy claims his old lady, they each get a tattoo of the other's name."

"Oh. Can I get that done?"

He nods. "I guess so. Run it by Axel or Grizz." He looks around the room. "They're probably busy," he mutters. "Take it to Fletch."

I spot him at the bar, and Coop leads me over. "Hey, brother, the Pres and VP are busy, but Xanthe wants her tattoo."

Fletch eyes me. "What if he doesn't remember?"

Coop groans. "Shit, brother, have some tact," he snaps.

"It's fine," I cut in before they can argue. "I want it anyway to prove I'm serious."

"There's a chance he'll make you cover it up if he decides not to pursue things," says Fletch gently. "Wouldn't you rather wait until he's feeling more like himself?"

I shake my head. "I feel so lost and alone right now. I need this to remind me what it's all for."

Fletch exhales, shrugging. "Okay. I'll get Ink to set up."

∽

WE USE AXEL'S OFFICE, AND I'M RELIEVED WHEN LEXI AND Gemma join me. "Usually, it's something you and your man do together," says Lexi, squeezing my hand. "But seeing as he's not here, we wanted to be here for you."

I nod. "I'd really like that." They settle on the couch, and I lie back in Ink's chair. "What's yours look like?" I ask, turning my head to the side to look at the girls.

The women exchange an amused look. "I didn't go traditional," says Lexi.

"What does that mean?" I ask. "Are there other ways to do this?"

She smirks. "Yes, but nothing you'd choose."

"I want to see."

She comes closer and lowers her top to show me the scarring on her chest. I wince, and she laughs. "Told yah."

"How was that done?"

"Branding iron," she says simply, and I gasp, horrified she'd do that to herself. "It's a long story. I'll tell you another time."

Ink sketches directly on my skin on the inside of my wrist. I smile, nodding in approval when he asks me to check. Then I close my eyes and leave him to get on with it. I think about Fury and everything we've been through. Our times together, both past and present, have been full of chaos and drama, and I find myself praying it's all worth it in the end. Because if I have to walk away after all this, it'll kill me.

The buzzing of the tattoo gun finally stops, and Ink wipes my skin. "All done," he announces, and I stare at the intricate lettering.

"I love it," I say with a smile. Even if I have to walk away, I'll always have a piece of him with me.

"Xanthe?" yells Grizz from upstairs. I frown, climbing from the chair and heading towards the stairs. "Xanthe, get the fuck up here now," he shouts, and I note the worry in his tone. I take the stairs two at a time until I'm standing in the doorway with everyone staring at Fury, who is holding his head like he's in pain.

"What's happened?" I ask, lingering in the doorway.

"You," whispers Fury, and his eyes burn into mine. I see that vulnerable boy I once knew and realise he's asking for me.

"Everyone out," I say, ignoring my racing heart. Nobody questions me as they file out, leaving us alone. I go over to the curtains and close them, blocking out the daylight. When I turn back to Fury, he looks lost, so I move closer to his bedside. "What do you need?" I ask gently.

This time, when his eyes find mine, there are tears glistening, and it breaks my heart. I don't speak because it's not words he needs right now. Instead, I climb onto the bed beside him and wrap my arms around his neck, pulling him against me. He doesn't fight me, instead pressing his nose against the crook of my neck and inhaling deeply.

A few minutes pass before I feel him relax against me and his breathing evens out. It would be easier to slip away and let him rest, but there's a selfish part of me that needs to feel him this close before he realises that he still doesn't remember me and pushes me away again. So, I settle for the uncomfortable position, with his calm breaths tickling my neck, and I close my eyes and drift off to sleep.

∽

I STIR, GROANING AS MY BODY ACHES IN PROTEST. MY LEGS HAVE gone dead because I stupidly tucked them under me, and my arm hurts from where it's tucked around Fury. I open one eye and realise he's awake. Feeling embarrassed, I try to sit up, only to realise he's holding my wrist. The one with the tattoo. *Fuck.* I didn't plan on letting him see it. At least, not yet.

"Sorry, it was a stupid idea," I mumble, trying to pull my arm free, but he grips it tighter. "You told Axel—"

"Mine," he whispers, running his thumb over the fresh ink.

"I know you probably said it to keep me safe," I continue, "but you told Chevy to tell Axel that I was yours."

"Sorry," he mutters.

I manage to sit up, freeing my arm and holding it protectively against my chest. *Is he sorry that he told Chevy that? Or sorry he can't remember?*

I slide from the bed. "You must be getting hungry," I say in a breezy tone. "I can fix you some food."

He gives his head a slight shake before muttering, "Toilet."

"Of course," I say. He eases himself to the edge of the bed

and waits a second before standing. I grip his arm to steady him, and we slowly walk towards the en suite. I wait just outside the door while he does what he needs to do, and then I walk him back to bed. Once he's sitting down, he takes my wrist again and runs his thumb over the tattoo. "Mine," he repeats.

"Food," I mutter, stepping away.

CHAPTER 17

Fury

Xanthe moves around the room like a ninja. She creeps around, checking my temperature, pulling the sheets over me, and just generally keeping a close eye on me, all while she thinks I'm sleeping. It's easier to lie here with my eyes closed than see the pain in hers whenever she looks at me.

I want to remember, but it doesn't matter how hard I try, I just can't. Not her or us, anyway. I do remember the fight, or parts of it. I keep seeing Jo's pleading eyes as she begs me to stop smashing my fist into Ripper's face. I also remember she's the fucking reason I'm here. She distracted me, probably on purpose to save her precious man. If only she knew the truth about him and everything he'd done.

The door opens, but I keep my eyes closed. Lying in this bed makes me feel weak and pathetic, and I don't need to see my brothers looking at me with pity.

"How's he doing?" It's Axel.

"Fine," Xanthe replies. It's the same reply she always gives, with her voice filled with sadness.

"Has he remembered anything?"

She scoffs. "If he has, he hasn't told me. But why would he? I'm just the nurse." My heart twists at her bitter words.

"Hey, you know that's not true, Xanth," Axel says, his tone laced with sympathy.

"Oh yeah?" she asks with an unamused laugh. "So, why does he pretend to be asleep whenever I'm in here?" *Fuck. My game's up.* The door opens and closes again, and I risk opening one eye to find Axel glaring at me. I shrug helplessly.

"She's finding it hard," he says.

"Me . . . too."

"We've made a decision," he continues. "We're ending Donnie and Ripper tonight." I growl in frustration, and Axel sighs. *They're mine to end.* "I know you want this, brother, but we can't keep them down there and risk them being found. Donnie's already been there a week." I turn my head away, done with this bullshit. "I know you're frustrated, brother, but as long as they're dead, what the fuck does it matter?"

∼

It's another hour before Xanthe returns to check me over. She's checking my pulse when I grab her wrist. She startles, inhaling sharply. "Donnie," I say, and she waits for me to continue. "I need . . . I want . . ." She continues to stare, and I'm getting pissed she's not helping me. I glare hard, but she continues to stare until I sigh in frustration.

"If you want to say something, say it," she snaps, and I arch a brow. Surely, that's not professional knowing my history. She rolls her eyes. "If you think I'm going to talk for you, think again. You want something, you fucking ask me." And then she continues to read my pulse.

I swallow, but as the words enter my head, they disappear

just as quickly. "Fuck," I yell, and she startles again then glares at me. "I want . . ." I growl, "to kill."

She almost smiles, shutting it down before it gets too wide. "Who?"

"Donnie."

"And how the hell do you plan to do that?" she asks, looking amused. It only annoys me more. "Besides, I thought Axel had taken care of him."

"Base . . . ment."

She glares at me. "What?" There's no way I'm repeating it. "Basement? Donnie is in the basement?"

I nod and add, "Ripper."

"You have to be shitting me," she snaps. "Why the hell are they down there, so close?"

"Help me."

She's already shaking her head. "No."

"Please."

"Absolutely not, Reese." Why does my heart swell whenever she says my real name like that? "You can just about walk to the bathroom without getting dizzy."

"Help me," I say more firmly.

"Let Axel deal with him."

"Xanth," I hiss, and this time, she smiles.

"You said my name."

I press my thumb over her tattoo. "Fury's property," I whisper. "Xanthe May Hart."

Her smile is the widest I've seen it. "That's the biggest sentence you've said since you woke."

"Help me," I repeat.

She groans. "How?" I haven't thought that far ahead, but she checks her watch. "The guys are in church. I could ask the women for help?"

I don't like the idea of involving them, but I won't make it that far without help, and Xanthe isn't strong enough to get me down to the basement. I nod, and she takes a breath.

"Okay, I'll be right back."

Xanthe

I FIND DUCHESS, LUNA, AND TESSA CHATTING IN THE BAR. I head over sheepishly, unsure how they'll react to my request. "How's he doing?" asks Luna.

"Good. He's saying a few more words."

"That's amazing news," Duchess replies.

"Actually, it's because of Fury that I'm here," I say, and they all stare at me. "I have the biggest favour to ask."

"Please let it be exciting. I am so bored," says Tessa.

"Fury wants to go down to the basement." They exchange wary looks. "He knows Donnie and Ripper are down there."

"Are they?" asks Luna.

I shrug. "Apparently."

"I wish they'd tell us stuff like that," she complains. "What if I went down there and stumbled across them?"

"Why would you go into the basement?" asks Duchess.

"The thing is, this is sort of time critical," I cut in. "Axel doesn't know, and they're all in church so . . ." I leave the sentence hanging.

Duchess is the first to stand. "I have a wheelchair," she tells me. "We can get him as far as the steps in that." I nod with a grin.

"I'm in. There's not much else to do," says Tessa.

"Great," I say. "Meet me back upstairs."

I find Fury standing, and I gasp. He shouldn't be doing that without someone here in case he collapses, but he's dressed in jeans and a shirt, and he already looks more like himself. I step closer, unable to stop staring at him. "I've got Duchess, Tessa, and Luna all in."

"Thank . . . you."

The door opens, and the three trail in. He takes one look at the wheelchair and shakes his head. "It's easier for us," I argue, "and quicker."

"As long as the lift doesn't get stuck. When was the last time that was used?" asked Luna.

"It works. I make the prospects check it all the time," Duchess replies. "Now, if you want to do this before church is done, you better get your backside in the chair so we can go."

He sighs before sitting in the chair. We take the lift and rush out the club before we're spotted. One of the prospects is outside on the gate and he saunters over. "Good to see you, man," he says to Fury.

"He needed some fresh air," I lie, continuing to push him around the back of the clubhouse.

We get to the basement doors, and Luna holds up a set of keys. I frown, and she smiles. "Grizz left them beside the bed."

She sets about trying various keys until the padlock clicks and opens. "Are you feeling okay to stand?" I ask Fury, and he nods, pushing to his feet but grabbing onto me for support.

Duchess moves the chair and takes his other arm. "What's the plan here?" she asks.

"He wants to talk," I lie, and Fury frowns at me. I didn't tell them the truth because I didn't think they'd help.

"Murder," he says, and Duchess rolls her eyes.

"How the hell are you gonna do that in this state?" she asks.

He grins. "Watch."

I turn back to Luna and Tessa. "If you help us get him down there, you can wait back up here. I don't want to involve you in anything."

Tessa scoffs. "Us old ladies stick together," she says firmly. "You asked for our help, so we're helping."

I smile with gratitude. "Thank you."

As we descend the steps one at a time, I screw my nose up at the damp stench. "It stinks down here," I whisper.

"Death," mutters Fury.

The first room we come to is empty, and Fury nods to the next. The cave-like doorways are low, and we bend to get through, finding Donnie tied to a chair. He's not as scary with his dirty clothes, his swollen face, and his head lolling to one side.

"Shall we wake him?" Luna whispers. Fury nods, letting go of me to hold onto the wall. Luna steps closer, glancing back with worry before gently poking his shoulder.

Duchess laughs. "Give him a good shake."

"I don't want to touch him," Luna hisses back. "Have you got a stick?"

I laugh, moving closer and grabbing Donnie's hair. "Wake the fuck up," I snap, and his eyes slowly open. "We brought you a visitor." My voice is strong, unlike usual, and I'm almost impressed with myself as I turn his head towards Fury.

Donnie sneers. "Aren't you a sight for sore eyes?" His voice is croaky from lack of water. I release his hair and step back.

Fury

I feel my chest swell with pride as Xanthe steps back, leaving room for me to step forward. "Are you hand delivering her to me?" he spits, looking Xanthe up and down.

I grip the knife tightly in my fist. "Mine," I growl, ramming it into his neck with force. The pain in my head intensifies, but I don't give in to it. I need this. I inhale the metallic aroma, feeling more like my old self. It's only when his gurgling stops that I open my eyes again and stare into his lifeless orbs.

I retrieve my knife, wiping his blood on my jeans before gripping hold of the damp wall to keep my balance. "Are you okay?" Xanthe whispers softly as she places her hand to my chest and stares into my eyes.

"Ripper," I mutter.

"Are you sure?" I nod once, and she exhales. "Okay." She slips her hand into my bloodied one and leads me towards the next room.

Ripper is awake and ready, smiling wide as we file in like fucking amateurs. He hasn't been down here long, his clothes still fresh, but he's taken a beating. "Thought your Pres would be the one to end me," he says.

"Surprise," I mutter.

"It's not even a fair fight," he argues. "Me tied up, you . . . slow."

My blood pumps faster, and I ball my fists in anger. "Was it a fair fight in the ring?" asks Xanthe. "Using your old lady to distract him?"

Ripper grins. "I'm so sad it's going to end like this, Xanthe. I had my eye on you."

She scoffs. "Like I'd give you a second look."

"Oh, I wasn't gonna get your consent," he sneers. "Where's the fun in that?"

That comment alone makes me realise the only place for the fucker is in the ground. I won't risk Xanthe. As I plunge the knife into his thigh, he laughs. "Just thinking about her tight little cunt is making me hard," he hisses, and I push the blade into his other thigh. "Bet she's a screamer," he continues, trying to push me into ending him quickly, but I won't. The fucker had my child killed. He beat Jo in front of the rest of the club. Pieces of my memory return like a slideshow—Jo curled in a ball crying while he beat on her, and me lying in a bloody mess on the floor, unable to fight back to avoid the wrath of my other brothers. I stab the blade into his shoulder, and this time, he growls.

"Die . . . slow," I hiss, stabbing his other shoulder before stepping back. His clothes are soaked in the blood pouring freely from his wounds. "Scum."

"You fucked my old lady," he yells angrily. "It should be you here."

"You beat . . . her."

"That's my business," he screams. "You don't get involved in another man's business."

"She deserves . . . better."

"She's a fucking whore," he shouts. "No wonder I beat her. After you left, I let my brothers fuck her too," he yells, and my blood runs cold. "For every day you were gone, she endured punishment. Slow, long, punishment."

"You're a monster," Xanthe whispers.

"No one makes me look a fool," he shouts.

Xanthe takes my hand. "You're doing that all by yourself," she says, leading me from the basement, followed by the others.

Axel rounds the corner, along with Grizz, just as I'm collapsing into the wheelchair. He stops in his tracks, staring at the blood on my clothes. "What the fuck have you done?"

"Holy shit," mutters Grizz.

"It was his kill," says Xanthe confidently, and I almost smile at the way she jumps to my defence. *Like a true old lady.*

"Did you witness it?" Grizz asks Luna.

"I closed my eyes," she says with a smirk.

"My office, now," Axel barks, turning on his heel and storming back inside. Grizz grabs Luna by the hand and drags her off.

"I think we're in trouble," Xanthe whispers in amusement.

Axel is pacing his office when we get inside. I get out the wheelchair and move to the couch while Xanthe stands by the door. "My . . . fault," I tell him.

"Oh, I know," snaps Axel. "But you didn't do it without

her," he adds, pointing to Xanthe. "To say you remember fuck all, you're making the perfect bloody team."

"He really should rest," Xanthe cuts in.

Axel's eyes narrow in on her. "I imagine a double murder takes it out a person."

"Exactly," she says brightly, ignoring his dangerously low tone. She heads for me, and Axel slams his hands on the desk, causing her to stop.

"You involved the women in club business," he growls. "You went against what I said," he adds.

Xanthe stares me in the eyes for a few seconds then something changes in her demeanour. She stands straighter and squares her shoulders while heading closer to the desk. I watch in astonishment as she places her hands on the edge and looks Axel dead in the eyes. "The women were very eager to help Fury get his revenge, so I don't regret it. After all, they have their own minds and can think for themselves. They were free to leave at any point. I just needed help getting Fury up and down the steps. I think you're pissed because Fury took matters into his own hands, but let's face it, they were going to die anyway, right?" When he doesn't answer, she nods. "That's what I thought. They deserved to die at the hands of Fury, and if it helps him to feel better about everything, then I, for one, am one hundred percent behind him."

My cock stirs, and I adjust myself to try to hide it. Fuck, she's hot when she's pissed. Even the Pres is stunned into silence. She turns on her heel, sending a smug smile my way before holding out her hand. I glance at Axel for permission, and he shrugs, clearly letting her attitude slide. We're almost at the door when he says, "For the record, you make one hell of an old lady."

CHAPTER 18

Xanthe

My heart is beating rapidly as I help Fury up the stairs to his room. When I finally look at him, he's smiling. "I always was good at getting us out of trouble," I say with a wink. "Now, let's get you out of these clothes."

I begin to undress him without thinking. He's capable of doing it himself, but he doesn't stop me, and as I shove his blood-soaked jeans down his thighs, his erection flops out proudly. I snigger, unable to hide my embarrassment. As a nurse, I've come face-to-face with my fair share of semis, and my professional side forces me to continue undressing him like it's no big deal. As I lift his shirt, he puts his arms up, and I remove it, leaving him completely naked. My cheeks are burning red because every part of me aches to touch him, but until he remembers us, I can't. It would feel too much like I was taking advantage.

"Shower," I prompt, stepping back.

"Help?" he asks.

I grin. "You just killed two men, so you can shower."

He hisses, holding his head, and I narrow my eyes, wondering if he's playing on it, but when he begins to bend at the waist, I hook an arm in his. "Fine. I'll stay in there with you." It's not like I haven't seen him naked. It's no big deal.

I turn the shower on, and we wait a few seconds until the steam billows out. Fury steps under the spray, and my eyes drift down to his now half-semi-erect cock. *At least it's deflating.* He grips the wall like he's struggling to stand, and I almost laugh at his poor attempt at acting. "I'm not helping you wash," I tell him firmly. "You're perfectly capable."

I take the shower gel from the shelf and hold it out to him. "And you're a terrible actor." He smirks, but instead of taking the gel, he grabs my wrist and tugs me to him. I crash against his wet chest and gasp as the water soaks my shirt.

"Help," he whispers, his lips a breath away from mine. We're locked in a stare as the water pours over us, and I feel his erection now pressing against my stomach. I swallow the huge lump of nerves in my throat.

"Fury," I whisper in a breathy tone.

"Mine," he replies, rubbing his thumb over my tattoo. "My Xanthe May." His lips gently brush over mine, and his hand travels up to cup my cheek as he tilts my head back slightly and deepens the kiss. It's slow, and he takes his time to slide his tongue against mine, occasionally nipping my lip the way he used to. I sigh happily that he's finally making a move.

When he pulls back, he rests his forehead against mine. "Help me . . . remember us."

His hands trail to my shoulders, and he begins to slide my top off. I release the buttons with shaking fingers, my mind racing. He lowers to his knees, wincing slightly before hooking his hands into my leggings and tugging them down my legs, taking my underwear with them. He throws my clothes out onto the tiled floor then takes both my hands and tugs me down onto his lap. He guides my legs to wrap around his waist, and his cock presses against me, standing proudly between us as he scoops his hands into my wet hair and pulls me in for another kiss.

His mouth travels down my chest and to my breast, taking my nipple into his mouth. I rest my hands behind me, closing my eyes as his tongue circles the bud. Pressing myself against his cock, I slowly drag my hips upwards before sliding back down. He groans, looking down between us and watching as I rub myself against him. Precum drips from him, and I gather it on my thumb, popping the digit in my mouth and sucking it clean. He watches through hooded eyes. "Condom," he mutters, glancing towards the draw under the sink.

I falter, his words hitting me like ice. Before the accident, he was all for unprotected sex, and now, he's insisting on protection. Instead, I slide my legs from around him and kneel before him, lowering my lips to his cock and taking him in my mouth. He needs a release, and I'm his old lady, whether he remembers or not. I've heard stories of the men turning to the club girls, and I won't let that happen.

I suck his cock like my life depends on it, wrapping my hands around the base and working him fast. It's minutes before he's growling his way through an intense orgasm. I pull back as streams of cum shoot out, covering my hand and dripping onto my leg.

I push to stand on shaky legs, wondering why the hell I feel like crying. I get out the shower and wash my hands in the sink, keeping my back to him while I compose myself. I'm not expecting his arms to wrap around my waist, and I jump with fright. He nuzzles his mouth against the crook of my neck, and I have the urge to shove him away. His hand travels down my stomach, but before it reaches its intended destination, I grab a towel and turn in his arms, forcing a smile. "Let's get you dried and back to bed."

His eyes narrow in confusion. "But . . . you," he says.

"I'm good," I say brightly.

~

I SPEND AN HOUR WATCHING FURY SLEEP. HE'S PEACEFUL FOR the first time since he came home. Usually, he fidgets and grumbles to himself, but tonight, he's sleeping like a baby. Maybe ending those fuckers has helped him.

I remove the shirt he gave me to wear once we got out the bathroom and head to my room, dressing in jeans and a shirt. And then I head downstairs, needing a drink.

Lexi is with Gemma, and when I approach, they make room at the bar, sliding along the seats and freeing the end one up for me. "We heard you yelled at Axel," whispers Gemma, smirking.

I scoff. "I didn't raise my voice once."

"True old lady style," says Lexi with a look of admiration.

"I doubt that," I mutter.

"Oh god, what's he done this time?" asks Gemma.

Fury

I'VE BEEN AWAKE FOR OVER AN HOUR AND THERE'S NO SIGN OF Xanthe. I throw my legs over the side of the bed and wait. It's like she has a sixth sense and usually comes running in at this point, but when the conjoining door doesn't open, I frown.

I go to the bathroom and stare at myself in the mirror. My bruises are a faded yellow now, almost fully healed, and yet here I am, still struggling to fucking talk. "Pussy," I say out loud, glaring at my reflection angrily. Maybe this is what Xanthe sees when she looks at me, cos she sure as hell doesn't see me as a man. She wouldn't even let me touch her earlier. It's like this wall came down between us.

My stomach growls with hunger, and I glance at my watch. It's almost seven, and Xanthe is never late with my food. She always brings me something at six.

I hear the bedroom door open and smile to myself. "Late," I call out, heading back into the room. I stop dead in my tracks at the blonde holding a tray of food. Disappointment fills me. *Where is she?*

"I'm Jennie," she says with a smirk. I glance down at my naked body and quickly grab a towel, holding it over my cock. She laughs. "Don't worry, big guy, I've seen it all before, even if you don't remember." She places the tray on the bed. "I can remind you, if you'd like," she adds, pouting slightly. "You said I had the best tits," she adds, lifting her shirt to show me her perky breasts. I glance away, my words clogging my throat. She seems to enjoy my discomfort and scoops some of the creamy dessert from my bowl, smearing it over her breast. "You enjoyed eating from them."

"What the fuck are you doing?" bellows Grizz, and I almost collapse in relief.

"Helping him remember the good times, VP," she says with a wink.

"Get the fuck out or I'll tell his old lady you were in here trying it on with her old man, and trust me, you don't want to get on Xanthe's wrong side."

Jennie rolls her eyes. "She's downstairs drinking the bar dry instead of taking care of her old man. I was just trying to help out."

"You're banned from coming in here again," he snaps, shoving her from the room as she wipes the cream with her finger and pops it in her mouth while laughing.

Grizz slams the door. "You can't be doing that shit now you got an old lady, brother. Axel don't allow that behaviour."

I shake my head. "I . . . didn't."

"I just came up to tell you he's dead. Ripper took his last breath five minutes ago."

"Good." I take a breath. "Where's Xanthe?" The words flow better than they have so far, and I relax a little. Maybe the harder I try, the worse it gets.

"She's downstairs, brother. Did you two argue or something? She's knocking shots back like water."

I shrug. "Take me to her," I force out.

He arches a brow. "If you're sure, but don't expect me to defend you. She's wild."

Xanthe and Lexi are singing badly through the karaoke machine, and I wince as the sound pierces my ears painfully. Grizz laughs, slapping me on the back. "Told yah."

"If you like it, then you shoulda put a ring on it," Xanthe yells into the microphone. "Don't be mad once you see that he want it."

"Is this a veiled message?" asks Coop, pointing to the nearest barstool. I shrug, taking a seat. My legs are shaking, and my head is throbbing. The last place I want to be is in here with all my brothers shooting me pitying looks.

"If you don't, you'll be alone, and like a ghost, I'll be gone," sings Xanthe.

"I'd say that was a woman's way of warning you, brother. What the hell did you do?" Coop continues.

"Nothing," I mutter.

"Drink?" asks the prospect from behind the bar. I catch the way Coop shakes his head, and I roll my eyes, turning back to watch Xanthe. She looks mad and, so far, hasn't seen me. Did she feel pressured earlier? *Fuck.* Did I force her? I give my head a shake to clear the image of her sucking my cock.

She jumps off the table and places the microphone down. *Thank fuck.* She takes a bottle of vodka from Luna and sips from it. I see the moment she spots me because she stills then almost chokes on her mouthful of vodka, spluttering violently before handing the bottle back to Luna.

Axel joins me. "Good to see you up and about, Fury."

"Is it?" I ask.

He follows my line of sight. "They're hard work," he says with a smirk, "but worth it."

"She's pissed," I mutter.

"Do you know why?" I shake my head, and he grins. "Yeah, that'll happen a lot."

"I need to . . . see . . ." I take a breath as Axel waits patiently. "Jo."

"Not a good idea. She goes to France tomorrow." I stare wide-eyed, and he shrugs. "I offered her a ticket to anywhere, and she chose France."

"He . . . Ripper . . . I remember things."

"About the fight?"

"Some . . . and when he . . . found out."

"Okay. So, why do you need to see her?"

"To say . . . sorry."

"Man, she doesn't need your apologies. She caused a whole lot of shit."

I shake my head. He wouldn't understand it, but she suffered badly while I just left. She deserves my apology. "Please."

He groans. "Fine. I'll have her here tomorrow before her train to France."

I push to stand. "I'm tired."

"You want me to get Xanthe?" he offers.

I glance to where she's chatting with Nyx and the other women. I don't like the way she leans in close to him, or how she occasionally glances my way to see if I've noticed. I shake my head. "No." I slowly head for the stairs then turn back to Axel. "If she wants . . ." I look over to her and Nyx again. "With Nyx."

"What the fuck are you talking about?" asks Axel.

"It's fine," I mutter, even though my heart aches. Of course, she's hot for a guy like Nyx. He can give her way more than I can. Besides, she can't stand to look at me, let alone have me touch her. "I'm good with it," I force out then leave.

Xanthe

Axel grabs the top of my arm, and I wince. "Hey," I cry as he takes the bottle from my hand.

"Axel," snaps Lexi, pushing to her feet.

"Your man is waiting for you," he spits angrily, guiding me towards the stairs.

I laugh, stumbling over my own feet. "My man," I repeat, laughing harder. He can't even stand me. "All I am is his nurse," I point out.

"Bullshit," he growls, grabbing my other arm and holding my wrist at eye-level. "Fury's property," he reads, shoving my arm away again like it offends him. He pushes me into his office, and I fall onto the couch. He grabs a bottle of water from the fridge and hands it to me. "You're a part of my club," he says firmly as I sit up, "and you're Fury's old lady. Behave like it."

My eyes widen. "Are you shitting me?" I snap. "I've been here the whole time," I scream. "Waiting for him to remember me like some sad little puppy dog waiting for any scraps he might throw my way." I burst into hot, angry tears, and Axel's scowl softens.

"I know this has been hard on you."

I bury my face in my hands, wiping my tears. "Every time we take a step forward, we take two back."

"That's normal in most relationships."

"It's just a lot," I whisper sadly.

"Yah know what he just said?" I shake my head. "He practically gave Nyx permission."

My heart aches. "So, what does that tell you, Axel? He's not interested in me."

"Nah, there was a look in his eye, Xanth, like he doesn't think he's good enough."

I roll my eyes and head for the door. "Goodnight."

CHAPTER 19

Fury

I waited, but she never came to check on me. I stare up at the ceiling, occasionally checking the clock. *Maybe she went after Nyx. Maybe Axel told her she could.* Why the fuck can't I just remember? I growl, hitting my fist into the mattress.

The door opens at exactly nine, and Xanthe saunters in looking fresh-faced as she places my tray on the bedside table. And suddenly, I feel a pang of jealousy. *What if she did fuck Nyx?* She certainly looks happier as she hums to herself while sorting my painkillers.

I push to sit, and she finally looks at me. "Good morning," she says with a smile. "Did you sleep well?"

"No," I grunt. Half my night was spent thinking about her, and the other half was picturing her and Nyx together.

"Shame. I can get you the sleeping tablets if you want them?" The last thing I want is to be back on the medication again after I've finally dropped to just a couple of painkillers. Deep down, I know I'd sleep better if she was beside me.

"Hangover?" I ask bitterly.

Her smile falters. "No."

"Did you . . . sleep well?"

"Like a baby," she replies, placing the pills in my hand and passing me the water. I throw them back without breaking eye contact. "Nyx?" I ask.

She frowns. "If you're asking me if I fucked Nyx," she snaps, placing her hand on her hip, "the answer is no." She takes the water from me. "Despite you giving me *permission*."

I can't deny I'm relieved. "You like . . . him."

"God, you're such a prick," she mutters, beginning to fold my clothes from last night and placing them in my drawers. "It's not like you want me."

"Mine," I snap.

She rolls her eyes. "You don't even remember, Reese." She sighs, pinching the bridge of her nose before running her hand over her tired face. "Look, I only moved in here because Donnie was looking for me, and he's no longer a threat, so I'm going to move back into my place."

My heart thumps heavily in my chest. I might not remember, but I know I don't want her to leave. "No."

"It's not up for discussion," she says sadly. "The doctor is coming to check on you later, and if everything's okay, I'm going home. You don't need me. You have your brothers to help."

The door opens, and Axel comes in. "Morning," he says, and Xanthe goes back to sorting my clothes. Jo appears in the doorway, and I wince. The timing is shit.

Xanthe turns just as Jo comes farther into the room, and her step falters. She inhales sharply, and I know she must have a million questions, but instead, she forces a smile. "I can see you have things to sort, so I'll be off." She avoids my eyes. "I'm meeting some friends for brunch, but Lexi is going to sort your lunchtime meds. I'll catch you later."

"Xanth," I say, my tone pleading, but she waves her hand dismissively.

"The doctor's coming at one. I'll make sure I'm back for then." And she rushes out.

Axel shifts uncomfortably. "Should I go talk to her?"

I shake my head. "She needs . . . space."

Axel gives a stiff nod. "Whatever you say. I'll let you talk." And then he leaves.

I pat the edge of the bed, and Jo lowers to sit. "How are you feeling?" she asks.

"Tired. Con . . . fused."

"Have you remembered anything?"

I nod. "Some things. Ripper said . . . he told . . . me." She stares down at her hands in her lap, and I place mine over hers. "I'm sorry."

When she looks up, there are tears in her eyes. "I'm sorry too. I should've left you well alone, Fury. Things were so hard with him, and you were a breath of fresh air. I didn't know he couldn't have kids, and when I got pregnant, I thought things would get better if he thought it was his kid. Maybe he'd stop beating me and," she sobs, "raping me."

My heart aches for her as she sobs silently. "After I left," I say.

She wipes her wet cheeks. "Things just got worse. He'd send in his men, one after the other . . ." She trails off. "He'd beat me until I was too terrified to move."

"Jo," I whisper.

"It's okay," she rushes to reassure me. "Axel gave me some money, and I'm going to stay with a friend. I can start my life again."

Her words make me feel a little better, and I smile. She leans closer, kissing me on the cheek. "I don't regret it," she whispers. "If we had happened in another life, I think I could've loved you." She stands. "Xanthe is a lucky woman. Treat her well, Fury."

Xanthe

"I'm not sure this is the answer," I say as Julianna tops up my wine glass.

"It's a boozy brunch, didn't I say?" she asks, laughing.

"You've been through a lot, and you deserve to unwind," adds Jorja.

"I think I'm gonna move out of the clubhouse."

"No," says Julianna. "Don't do that."

"It was temporary," I say. "I'm not even sure any of it would've happened had it not been for Donnie."

"Don't say that," she whines. "You two are my favourite love story."

"Love?" I scoff. "We're not in love."

"You forget we know you," says Jorja. "Stop lying to yourself."

I take a large gulp of wine. "It's pointless, anyway. He clearly doesn't feel the same."

"Why are you so worried about making him remember?" asks Julianna.

"True love doesn't burn out. He'll fall in love all over again," adds Jorja.

"If you stick around and show him how amazing you are," Julianna finishes.

"I've made up my mind. I'm going home. If it's true love like you say, it'll happen anyway, whether I'm there or not."

"You're here drowning your sorrows with us while this Jo woman is with your man."

The thought makes me sick. "He's not my man. Not anymore."

"Honestly, this self-pity doesn't suit you," says Jorja, and my mouth drops open.

"I'm having a moment here."

"You literally went cold on him because he asked to use protection," she states. "And I don't see what's wrong with that."

I groan dramatically. "You don't understand how he was before."

"And shit's changed," says Jorja firmly. "But you haven't. It must be so damn scary for him to wake up and have no idea what's been happening in his life these last few months."

I finish my glass of wine. "I came out to forget. Now, cheer me up instead of judging."

Fury

I CHECK MY WATCH AGAIN. IT'S BEEN TWO MINUTES SINCE I LAST looked, and the doctor smiles awkwardly. "Maybe just tell me," suggests Jennie. "I'll pass it on to his nurse."

I want to scream. She knows damn well Xanthe is more than my nurse, but fuck, why the hell isn't she here? Jennie was like a cat that got the cream the second she realised Xanthe wasn't around, and I need someone here in case I forget what the doc tells me. The doctor is looking at me for confirmation, so I give a nod.

Minutes later, he smiles and holds out a hand for me to shake. I reach for it, realising I haven't heard a thing he's said. "It's been a pleasure, and in the nicest possible way, let's hope we don't meet again." He laughs at his own joke. "My colleague will be in touch to check in with you regarding any lasting damage."

Jennie shows him out, and when she returns, I'm already out of bed. I'm over sitting around all day. I'll never get better doing nothing.

"I know he said you're on the mend, Fury, but I still don't think you should rush into anything."

"Xanthe?" I ask.

"I don't know where she is," she says and almost looks sorry for me.

I take my mobile from the bedside table and dial her number. *What if something happened to her?* My heartrate spikes at the thought. "I'm sure she's fine. She's a big girl."

I roll my eyes and pass her, heading downstairs. The men are just coming out of church, and Grizz frowns when he sees me. "You okay?"

"Xanthe."

"What, she isn't back?" I shake my head. "Did she say where she was going?"

"Brunch," I mutter, angry that I didn't ask for details.

"Look, it's only been a couple hours. She'll be back." He pats me on the shoulder, and the urge to snap his fingers is strong. I'm sick of patronising comments and sympathetic looks. I want her home now. As if my prayers are answered, the door opens and Xanthe stumbles in. She giggles, looking up in surprise at the bikers in the room.

"Aww, guys, is this my leaving party?" she slurs, and my blood boils. I was worried sick, and she was out getting drunk . . . again. She crashes against Nyx, throwing her arms around him and grinning like a fool. Nyx tries desperately to free himself, and she laughs harder. "Fury doesn't care," she whispers loudly enough for everyone to hear. "He said you could fuck me."

The men move aside, and she spots me. Nyx steps away, and she stumbles again, almost falling to her knees. "I'm sorry, brother," mutters Nyx, stuffing his hands in his pockets.

It's the final straw. *More apologies. More sympathy.* I roar angrily with frustration, batting a chair to the side and sending it flying across the room. *I just want to fucking remember.* I sweep my hand across a table, sending glasses to the floor. Weeks of pent-up aggression burst from me, and each cry of anger leaves my throat raw. When Axel finally rushes me from behind and wraps his arms around me, holding my arms by my side, I look up to see absolute terror on Xanthe's face. Her hands are over her mouth, and her eyes are wide in shock. Tears are streaming down her face, but at least she doesn't look at me with sympathy.

I pant heavily, and Axel loosens his grip, realising I have no more strength in me. The door opens, and Dianna enters, humming to herself. She looks at the mess before her, her eyes going around the room and taking in the utter shock on everyone's faces, and then she places her bag on the floor and says, "Somebody put the kettle on. I'll take it from here."

"Mum, I don't think that's a good idea," Xanthe begins, but Dianna holds her hand up to stop her speaking.

"Everyone can leave. I'll be fine with Reese."

The men begin to file out. Axel asks her how she takes her tea then disappears into the kitchen. There's just me, Xanthe, and Dianna remaining, and suddenly, all I want to do is cry. *Fuck.* I haven't cried in such a long time. Not properly, anyway. Somehow, I can always turn it off.

"Xanthe, that includes you," she says firmly.

Xanthe goes to pass me, and I take her wrist, pressing my thumb to her tattoo. "Mine," I whisper. She doesn't make eye contact, instead staring at the ground before pulling free and going upstairs.

"I can't sit in this mess," mutters Dianna, shaking her head. "Let's clean it up." She picks up a chair, and I take the sweeping brush that's resting against the wall and begin to sweep the broken glass. My entire body aches, and my head thumps painfully. "Bursts of anger are normal with a brain injury," she adds, sweeping some shards of glass from the table, "but this behaviour isn't acceptable." She busies herself with the cushions on the sofa, shaking each one out. "You've been through a lot, but lots of people have and they don't smash things up." I feel like a naughty schoolboy, and I almost smile. "I don't know what you find so funny," she mutters. "You know how I feel about violence." She heads over to the bar and grabs a dustpan and the bin.

Axel returns holding a cup of tea. "I had to make it," he says, looking confused. "There was no one around to do it."

"Do you own this establishment?" Dianna asks.

"Yes, ma'am," he says proudly.

"You'd better work out how much he owes for the damage."

Axel grins, patting me on the back, "I'll let him off. He ain't the first brother to break sh- things," he corrects before cursing. He leans in closer to me. "She clipped me around the ear when you were in hospital for swearing," he whispers with a laugh. "I'll be in my office if you need anything," he offers before heading off.

Dianna holds the dustpan, waiting for me to sweep up the broken glass, then she pours it in the bin. "I thought I'd come and stay for a few weeks," she announces, brushing her hands down her dress and heading for the couch. She pats the space beside her, and I join her. "I had a feeling Xanthe needed me, but maybe it was you?"

Coop wanders in, stopping when he lays his eyes on Dianna. A smile creeps over his face. "Well, hello. I don't believe we've met." She stands to shake his offered hand, and she's equally as smiley. I roll my eyes.

"I'm Xanthe's mother, Dianna."

"Beautiful name for a beautiful lady."

I scoff, and Coop releases her hand. "I'll leave you two alone. Just call if you need anything at all," he adds.

"He seems charming," she gushes, staring after him. I narrow my eyes, and she composes herself. "Do you remember the first night you came to us? It was late, and I'd had dinner waiting for you at six because the social worker said she'd get you there for then, only she went to get you and you'd run away. Mack said right then he didn't think we'd be a good fit. We were already struggling with Xanthe's behaviour."

"You should have . . . listened to him." The flow of my words feels better. Maybe the blowout was exactly what I needed.

She smirks. "I was never one to back down from a challenge, you know that."

"You . . . did, though," I remind her, "in the . . . end."

She gives me a sad smile. "When you have your own children, you'll understand it, especially if she's a girl. I love every single child who came through my door, Reese. It wasn't very often I wanted to hold on to them forever. But you," she looks me in the eyes, "there was something about you."

"It was an . . . act," I say with a shrug. "I was . . . tired of being . . . moved on."

She gives her head a knowing shake. "When you finally walked through my door, you looked at the roast dinner I'd set out for you, and I could see you wanted to smile. Instead, you said—"

"That looks . . . like shit," I cut in, and we both smile. "I was so . . . rude and so . . . ungrateful."

"You were a teenage boy afraid of rejection. Any time we did anything nice, it was met with anger. And that wasn't a reflection on you but how you'd been treated." She places her hand in mine. "You soon settled down, and Mack realised he was wrong about you. You were good for Xanthe. You kept her on track."

"I didn't," I protest.

"You did, Reese. Before you, she felt a little lost and got in with the wrong crowd. You made her see how bad they were for her. We started to see glimpses of our happy little girl again. You did that."

I pull my hand free. "I fell in love . . . with her. I ruined it."

"We ruined it, not you, not Xanthe." She sighs heavily. "I think back to those days so much and I wish I'd never told Mack what I suspected. If I'd have just kept my mouth shut, you wouldn't have been sent away."

"We can't change . . . the past," I say.

"But we can change the future," she declares. "Xanthe loves you so much."

"She's mad I . . . don't remember," I mutter.

"What is there to remember? You'd only just met back up really. You both just need to get back to that point."

"How?" I ask. "I see how much . . . love she's got for me, the way she . . . looks at me like . . . I'm her life, and I feel so…"

CHAPTER 20

Xanthe

I stand awkwardly in the doorway, staring wide-eyed at Fury, and it's like all my fears are confirmed in that one sentence. It's Mum who spots me, clapping her hand over his to shut him up. But it's too late—I heard the part that mattered, even if he didn't finish the words.

"I just came to say your room is ready," I say, forcing a smile.

Fury jumps up, rushing towards me. "Shit, Xanthe, let . . . me finish."

"It's fine," I say a little too brightly, turning on my heel. Fuck, if he touches me, I'll crumble. I take the stairs two at a time. "Could you show Mum to the top floor?" I throw over my shoulder. "I just remembered I have something to do."

I burst into my bedroom and slam the door closed, leaning against it. My heart is pounding, and I feel sick. He must think I'm such a desperate, sad act. I turn the lock and then pull a bag from under my bed. I was so certain I wanted to leave earlier, but after chatting with the girls and having one too many drinks, I'd softened a little, thinking maybe I should just stick around and see what happens. But I can't now. Not after hearing him confess that he doesn't feel the same.

I pull my clothes from the drawers and stuff them into the bag, not caring if they're crumpled. He taps lightly on the door, and I pause, holding my breath. I know it's him just by the way he knocks. *How sad is that?* "Yeah?" I call, keeping my voice even.

"Can we talk?" he asks through the door.

"Now isn't a good time. Maybe tomorrow?"

"But you didn't let . . . me finish."

"Finish what?" I ask calmly, going over to my dresser and sweeping all my products into my vanity bag.

"Let's not pretend you . . . didn't hear me."

"I'd prefer to," I say with a small, unamused laugh. "I'm tired, and I need to sleep the wine off. I'll come and find you later."

"Yah know, it's an old . . . lady's duty to listen to . . . her man," he says.

My heart twists, and tears fill my eyes. "I'm not your old lady."

It's met with silence. At least he's got the message. After a few seconds, I stuff the rest of my things into the bag and zip it up. I glance around the room to check for anything, and that's when I see him standing in the conjoining doorway, watching me. His eyes fall to the bag and then back to me. "You didn't lock . . . this one," he says.

My adrenaline spikes, making my sickness worse. "I can see that," I mutter, stuffing my feet into my trainers. "I'm just gonna go," I add, grabbing my coat. "And it would be so much easier on my heart if you just let me." A lone tear falls down my cheek.

"I was so fucking . . . mad when you didn't . . . show earlier." I resist the urge to roll my eyes. Nurse duties are done, I thought he'd realise that by now. "I wanted you . . . here when the doctor came."

"There are plenty of people round to support you," I mutter.

"They're not you," he says, stepping closer.

"And Mum will stick around for a while. She'll love fussing over you."

"I don't want her to . . . fuss over me," he says, gently taking my chin in his fingers and tipping my head back to look him in the eye. "I want you."

"I can't," I whisper, my voice breaking with emotion.

"Why?"

"It's too hard."

He presses his thumb over my tattoo. "Mine." I shake my head slightly, and his eyes darken. "Mine," he repeats more firmly.

"You have no idea how hard it is," I say, allowing the tears to roll down my cheeks. "To love someone so much and be met with nothing."

"Baby, I grew up knowing that . . . feeling all too well. But that . . . isn't what this is."

"Isn't it?" I demand, taking a step back so his hands fall away. "I can't sit here waiting for you to remember how you felt. If you even fucking felt it. I don't know if you were serious because you left and came back another person." His head bows, and his hands hang limply by his sides. I'm reminded again of the little boy I used to know, and it breaks my heart. "I have to put me first," I add sadly.

"I feel different," he mutters. "Angrier, more tired . . . impatient. But one thing that . . . hasn't changed, Xanth, is how I feel . . . about you." He looks me in the eye, and I hold my breath, unsure of what he's about to say. "From the second I saw you in that . . . stupid bright trainers with your . . . sprayed hair, I loved you." I inhale sharply. It's the same thing he said to me before the accident. "You went to that nineties . . . party, and I spent the fucking . . . night looking out the window, wondering if you . . . were okay. Stressed some teenage fucker . . . had his hands in your pants."

I give a watery smile. "I was jealous . . . over a girl I didn't even know. But we went . . . on to have the best two years . . . of my life. I'd never felt so loved and needed. When . . . I left, I was more broken than I'd ever been . . . and I never felt fixed after you. Until now. And I might not remember . . . coming to the hospital and being patched up. I might . . . not remember our conversation or how I made . . . you go out for coffee. But I am one hundred percent . . . certain that I fell in love with you . . . all over again. Because I never stopped, Xanth. You have always owned my heart."

"But you . . ." I frown. "You told Mum—"

"You didn't let me finish. I was about to say . . . I feel so inadequate. You look at me like I'm your lifeline . . . and all I've done is bring you stress and misery. Before me . . . you had a good life, just like before, and I come along and fuck it all up."

I shake my head, closing the gap between us. "You're wrong," I tell him, placing my hand on his cheek. "You are my life, Reese. Without you, it's pointless."

He smiles. "Please stay."

I give a small laugh. "I was all packed, ready for my dramatic exit."

"There was no way . . . I was gonna let you leave."

"No?"

He shakes his head and places a gentle kiss on my lips. "And if you ever . . . go off radar again, I'll tear the . . . town up looking for you."

"I lost track of time," I say, smirking.

"Well, Jennie was eager . . . to play nurse."

I laugh. "Why does she terrify you so much? You and her had a thing," I remind him but before I can finish, he kisses me hard, holding me tightly.

"Some memories are . . . best left forgotten."

Fury

"Unpack," I tell her, swatting her on the backside. "I want to take you . . . out for food."

"Really?" she asks, laughing. "That's what you want to do right now?"

I grin, knowing exactly where her mind is at. "Donnie isn't a threat . . . now, so I want to walk freely . . . with my woman."

She bites her lower lip and smiles coyly. "That's kind of cute, so I'll keep my smutty suggestions to myself."

I arch a brow. "Save them for . . . later."

We go downstairs hand-in-hand. Axel looks over from where he's got Lexi backed up against the wall. "Finally," he says with a wink.

"You sorted it?" asks Lexi, grinning wide, and I nod. "We should celebrate."

"Not so fast, Mouse. We're in the middle of something," Axel cuts in, gently gripping her throat and nipping her lower lip.

Dianna is lost in conversation with Coop, and I narrow my eyes. "Watch him," I tell Xanthe.

"Aww, I like Coop," she replies.

"As a stepdad?" I ask, and she laughs.

"I'll be Lexi's sister."

We head out to my bike, and I take a deep breath. The doctor gave me the all-clear to drive when I feel ready, but it's the first time since the accident, and I can't pretend I'm not nervous. As if she senses it, she squeezes my hand. "You've got this."

I take her helmet and push it on her head, fastening the strap. I throw my leg over the beast and carefully put my own helmet on as Xanthe slides on behind me. She wraps her arms around me, and it's the best feeling.

I start the engine, and my entire body relaxes. For the first time in weeks, I feel like my old self, and as we pull out onto the road, it's as if nothing ever happened. The rumble of the engine is all the medicine I needed.

Ten minutes later, I park the bike up in a quieter part of town and remove my helmet. When I first arrived in London, I came to this restaurant for a traditional curry, and when I opened my eyes after the accident, it's one of the few things I remembered. I tell Xanthe the story as we enter hand-in-hand.

Once we're seated and have placed our order, I take her hands across the table, tracing my thumb over her tattoo. "I need one."

"I've never had my name on anyone's skin before," she says thoughtfully.

"Good."

"I know this is a huge thing for you," she adds, "but I was thinking, maybe we could get married."

"If that's what . . . you want."

She stares open-mouthed, "Really?" I nod. "But you didn't seem keen before . . ." She trails off, realising I don't remember, and I smile.

"I was an . . . idiot before. Now, I will do . . . anything to make you happy."

"It doesn't have to be a big one, or even soon, just one day."

But I'm already thinking of ways to get her up the aisle soon. "Kids?" I ask. It's not something I've ever thought about. When Jo got pregnant, I was terrified. After my childhood, why wouldn't I be? But Xanthe is different, and with her help, I know I'd be a good dad.

"I always said I didn't want them," she says, and my heart drops, "but when I imagine you holding our baby, it makes me feel differently."

I grin. "Good, cos I wasn't waiting for . . . your consent. We're having babies."

"Babies?" she repeats, laughing. "As in more than one?"

I nod. "There won't ever be a time . . . when you're not filled with . . . my babies."

She leans over the table, hooking her hand around my neck and pulling me closer for a kiss. "At least we get to practise a lot."

"First, we eat," I whisper against her lips. "You need to be . . . strong if you're going to be a . . . mum to a football team."

She sits back in her seat. "Imagine Mum with grandbabies."

"She will need to . . . be closer."

"She's not that far from us," says Xanthe.

"I was thinking she could . . . move into the clubhouse."

Xanthe stares wide-eyed. "You want my mother to move into the clubhouse?" I nod. "Why?"

"I don't like the . . . thought of her being alone."

Xanthe's face softens. "You're too cute."

"Don't tell my brothers."

EPILOGUE

Xanthe
Six months later . . .

I carefully back out the room without Lexi or Luna noticing. I love them both, but I need to see Fury, and they've specifically banned all contact until the morning when we say our vows.

I rush out the hut and race across the damp grass. We chose to have our wedding in a wonderful place set in the idyllic countryside. We booked all their huts for the entire weekend, and some of the bikers brought tents to camp because there wasn't enough room for us all.

I reach Fury's hut and tap on the door. He swings it open wrapped in a towel, his body wet, and I arch a brow. "You better be alone in there."

He smirks, reaching for me and dragging me in before Axel sees, as he is under strict instructions from Lexi to keep us apart. "I was just thinking about you."

NICOLA JANE

I smile smugly, ripping his towel away and eyeing up his huge erection. "And here I am, at your service."

"Did anyone tell you that you have the best timing?" he growls, lifting me in his arms and pushing me against the wall. "But if you ever sneak out in nothing but underwear again, I'll be pissed." He moves my panties to one side and sinks into me. I dig my nails into his shoulders. I can't get enough of him. It's been six months since he caught me leaving, and we've not been apart since. Wherever I am, so is he, and vice versa. The only place I can't go is church, but luckily, I have my girls there to hang out with. And although Fury's recovery took some time, he's almost back to his old self. His speech is perfect, but he'll never fight again, though I'm not sad about it, even if it did take him some time to get used to the idea.

"We need to be fast," I pant.

"The first time," he whispers, nipping my neck.

I giggle. "They'll come looking for me."

"Let them," he whispers against my clammy skin. "Now I have you here, you ain't leaving until it's time to get into that very expensive wedding dress." He didn't see the point in spending so much on a dress when he planned to rip it off right after the wedding. I had a real job convincing him it's not all about the wedding night.

I feel my orgasm building, and Fury moves faster, chasing his own release. He doesn't stop when Lexi bangs on the door. "Xanthe May Hart, get out here right now."

"Oh shit," I whisper as the first shudders of pleasure rip through me. Fury places his hand over my mouth, thrusting harder.

"Are you having sex?" she demands.

I can't help the laugh that escapes me. "Shhh," he growls in my ear.

He closes his eyes, gently wrapping his hand around my

throat as he comes apart, growling loud enough to be heard by anyone outside.

I hear Lexi calling for Axel. "Where's the fire?" he asks, joining her outside the door.

"You had one job," she snaps, "and now, my bride is in with the groom."

Fury carries me over to his bed, laying me down and kissing me until my toes curl. This is all part of his continued plan to get me pregnant. Luna jokes that he'll be holding my legs up in the air soon if I don't catch. It's a strong possibility, but I don't mind at all because having our own little family is all we both want.

Fury

THE CEREMONY IS OVER QUICKLY, WHICH I'M GLAD ABOUT because all I can think about is being alone with my wife. *My wife.* Fuck, that sounds good.

When I saw Xanthe walking down the aisle towards me, I forgot how to breathe. She'd have had that effect on me no matter what she wore, but the stunning cream-coloured dress that sparkled with each step was breathtaking. She is every bit the princess in our story, and my first thought was, fuck, she's all mine, followed by how I can't wait to see how beautiful she'll look carrying my baby. And if I have my way, that'll be any day now.

"Dance with me, wife," I whisper in her ear, interrupting her conversation with Luna.

Her smile is instant, and I pray she reacts like that every time she sees me for many years to come, because making her happy is all I want.

She slips her tiny hand into mine, and I lead her to the crowded dance floor. Wrapping her in my arms, I stare down at her, admiring her beauty. "I can't believe we actually got married," she says.

"Together forever," I reply, kissing her gently.

"I'm so happy."

"Me too."

"I notice Mum and Coop seem to be hitting it off," she adds, and I glance over to where the old bastard is twirling Dianna around nearby. I roll my eyes, and Xanthe laughs. "As long as she's happy."

The song comes to an end, and before the next starts, I pull her even closer. "I don't think anyone will notice if we slip off."

Xanthe giggles, but I know she's thinking the same. "Fine, but if Lexi comes looking for us, you can deal with her." I made sure Axel was keeping Lexi busy for this exact reason.

Since Xanthe came back into my life, we've not had it easy, but we didn't give up on each other. She stuck by me through the hardest days of my life, even when I tried to push her away. And somehow, every day since then, she's made me feel like the most important man in the world . . . like I'm worthwhile. And when we have a family of our own, I'll be part of something I've spent my entire life craving.

We were always meant to be. Set in stone to last forever.

FOLLOW NICOLA HERE...

I love to hear from my readers and if you'd like to get in touch, you can find me here . . .

My Facebook Page
My Facebook Readers Group
Bookbub
Instagram
Goodreads
Amazon
I'm also on Tiktok

Printed in Dunstable, United Kingdom